"You set me up, Jenna. Why?" he demanded. "What's in it for you?"

She blinked. "I had no idea you were on the case, Lex."

He cupped her jaw, tilted it brusquely up. "Don't give me the bimbo spiel, Ms. Rothchild. If you're trying to mess with this case because you have something to hide, I promise you now, I *will* find it."

She swallowed, pupils darkening reflexively. "You still owe me a date, Lex."

"I owe you nothing, Jenna."

"Not to my mind. And if you don't play, agent, I don't give." She made a moue, and all he could think about was kissing those full, pouty red lips of hers.

Lex swallowed against the dryness in his throat. And before re-engaging his brain, the words came out of his mouth. "One date. That's it. The money goes to charity. Then this is done. Over. *Capiche?*"

"What ever made you think I wanted—" her eyes teased slowly over his bare chest, "—anything more?"

Dear Reader,

Magic happens in Vegas. It's what the place sells—Luck, Fate, a chance to win a dream with the simple flick of a card, the pull of a handle, the roll of dice.

Such is the seduction of Sin City. And therein lies the danger.

The allure of the infamous Rothchild diamond, The Tears of the Quetzal, is no different. In the right hands, the Quetzal promises enduring love. But as we have seen in the LOVE IN 60 SECONDS series, in the wrong hands, grave misfortune is sure to follow. Whether the mysterious Mayan rock actually alters the destiny of those whose path it crosses is immaterial. Because like Vegas, the Quetzal opens the heart to the possibility of magic. And like Vegas, it can also destroy.

I hope you enjoy the manner in which this bewitching diamond entwines the lives of a rather unlikely couple—cool, buttoned-up FBI agent, Lex Duncan, and hot young casino heiress, Jenna Jayne Rothchild. But before they can find true love, Lex will need to open his heart to the possibility that even he, an orphan, can find family. In Vegas.

Loreth Anne White

LORETH ANNE WHITE

Her 24-Hour Protector

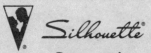

Romantic
SUSPENSE

Special thanks and acknowledgment to
Loreth Anne White for her contribution to the
Love in 60 Seconds miniseries

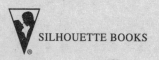 SILHOUETTE BOOKS

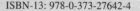

ISBN-13: 978-0-373-27642-4

HER 24-HOUR PROTECTOR

Copyright © 2009 by Harlequin Books S.A.

Visit Silhouette Books at www.eHarlequin.com

Printed in U.S.A.

Books by Loreth Anne White

Silhouette Romantic Suspense

LORETH ANNE WHITE

was born and raised in southern Africa, but now lives in Whistler, a ski resort in the moody British Columbian Coast Mountain range. It's a place of vast, wild and often dangerous mountains, larger-than-life characters, epic adventure and romance—the perfect place to escape reality.

It's no wonder it was here she was inspired to abandon a sixteen-year career as a journalist to escape into a world of romantic fiction filled with dangerous men and adventurous women.

When she's not writing, you will find her long-distance running, biking or skiing on the trails, and generally trying to avoid the bears—albeit not very successfully. She calls this work, because it's when the best ideas come.

For a peek into her world visit her Web site at www.lorethannewhite.com. She'd love to hear from you.

Prologue

The Nevada night was hot—no air-conditioning.

Lex clutched his teddy against his tummy even though it made him hotter, but he liked to hold his bear close when this particular TV program was on because sometimes the show made him scared. He was perched on the edge of his mom's bed wearing only his jammie shorts while he watched. His mother sat farther up, by the pillows, emptying the fat brown envelope that the man brought once a month.

Lex glanced at her during the commercial. She was counting out the cash onto the bed cover. His mom was always happy when the money came. She said it helped boost her croupier's income from the casino. Tomorrow she'd take him to the burger place for a special kids meal with a toy. It was their routine the day after the envelope arrived. Lex hoped that maybe when he turned six she'd take him to the steak house instead, where the chef cooked over big orange flames. He didn't need toys in his meal anymore, but he didn't want to tell her and hurt her feelings. He loved his mom. She was the prettiest woman he'd ever seen, too.

She caught him watching and smiled. He grinned back, getting that silly squeeze in his chest. But before he could turn back to his TV show, there was a crash downstairs in the hall. His mother tensed.

That made Lex scared.

A man's voice reached up the stairs. "Where's the kid, Sara!"

His mother's face went sheet-white. She pressed her index finger over her lips, telling Lex to stay quiet. Then she quickly gathered the money, reached for her purse and removed a small gun. Lex stared at it. His heart started to beat really fast. He clutched Mr. Teddy tighter.

"Where's the damn kid, Sara?" The voice—rough and raspy like Velcro tearing—was coming up the stairs. "He wants the boy!"

Lex's mother took his arm, dragged him to the closet. She got down to his eye level, grasped his shoulders tight. "Lexington," she whispered. She only called him Lexington when something was very serious, or he'd done something very wrong. "You get in that closet, d'you hear? Get in right behind the clothes. No matter what, do *not* move. Do *not* come out—"

"Sara!"

She shoved him quickly into the dark closet, shut the door, locked it. Lex peered through the louvered slats, but he could only see the bottom half of the room because of the way the slats were angled. He saw his mother's hand grabbing the telephone next to her bed.

The bedroom door crashed back against the wall. His mother screamed, aimed her gun at the man with one hand, holding the phone in her other. "Stay back! I'm calling the cops." She started to dial. That's when he heard the man hit his mother. A horrible sort of wet, crunching sound.

His mother gasped, dropping the receiver as she crumpled to the floor. Lex heard the gun skitter under the bed.

The man's hand—tanned with lots of dark hair on it—reached down and jerked the phone cord out of the wall. "Where is the damn kid, Sara?" he growled. Lex saw a knife glinting in his hand but couldn't see his top half, just his checkered pants.

"He…he's not here…" His mom was sobbing on the floor behind the bed. "I swear he's not."

"Lying bitch. I'll find him." He started to come toward the closet. Lex's little limbs began to shake. He wanted to smash out of the closet and kick the balls off that man, but he couldn't move.

"No! Please! He's not here!" He saw his mother had her gun again. She was on her knees by the bed. Her face was wet from tears. She aimed at the man, her hands shaking, and Lex heard a gunshot.

The man jerked, stumbled, swore something awful. "You… *shot me.*" He lunged forward, grabbed his mother by her hair and he cut his mother's throat. Blood went everywhere. Lex dropped Mr. Teddy and scooted right to the back, pulling his mother's dresses over him. He squeezed his eyes very tight, trying to shut out what he'd seen.

He heard the man's footsteps coming back to the closet. The door rattled, and Lex peed his pants. Then he heard police sirens—his mother's 911 call must have gone though. The man swore, staggered wildly out of the room. Lex heard tires screeching.

It fell silent in the room for a while before Lex heard the sirens growing really loud and stopping outside. There was noise again, lots of noise, all muddled up and not making sense—footsteps, yelling for paramedics. The girl from upstairs was sobbing, saying she'd heard fighting, a gunshot, someone running, a car fleeing. Then a male voice, deep like a drum, said an ambulance was no use.

His mother was dead.

Lex's whole body went cold, like ice. He couldn't think anymore. A big shadow came toward the closet door. And a little squeak of terror escaped Lex's chest as the door was rattled again. Someone said something about a key on the body. The door was unlocked, pulled open and the dresses covering him were yanked aside.

He blinked up into the sudden white glare of lights, saw the policeman's badge.

And that's how the cops found him. Stuffed into the back of the closet behind his mother's clothes. Mute with shock.

It took a full year before Lex could speak again. But his mother never came back.

And the police never found the man who'd cut his mother's throat.

Lex, however, would never, ever forget his voice. And he swore that one day he'd find that man. He would make him pay for what he'd done to his beautiful mother.

Chapter 1

FBI Special Agent Lex Duncan was due on stage right after the Vegas investment banker who was strutting down the runway with a long-stemmed rose clenched between his straight white teeth.

"Now this, ladies—" crooned the Bachelor Auction for Orphans emcee, a popular Las Vegas television host with dulcet tones of honey over gravel and butter-gold hair to match "—is an investment banker with *mutual* interest in mind. What red-blooded woman wouldn't want this macho money man to manage her *assets* for the night? Who knows, ladies—" the emcee lowered her voice conspiratorially. "There might just be some long-term profit for the right bidder…"

Shrieks and hoots erupted from the invitation-only crowd of almost one thousand very well-heeled Las Vegas women as Mr. Investment Banker shucked his pin-striped jacket, peeled off his crisply ironed shirt and got busy showing off some serious sweat equity of his own, obviously earned by heavy capital investment in the gym. The bids started, kettle drums rolling softly in the background heightening the tension.

Lex swore and shot a desperate glance toward the glowing red Exit sign backstage. He felt edgier now than he had during his first FBI takedown of a violent felon. Somehow he'd ended up being slated as the last bachelor up for grabs tonight, and he was feeling the pressure. The men ahead of him had already driven bids all the way up to a whopping $50,000, which went to a rugged foreign correspondent whose "sword" was apparently mightier than his pen—a comment that had brought the house down as the evening eased into night, laughter oiled by the complimentary cocktails that were loosening the ladies' designer purse strings and heating libidos.

Whoever had staged this event in Las Vegas's legendary Ruby Room with its massive art deco clock, shimmering chandeliers, red tones and old black-and-white photos that alluded to the thrilling mystique of Vegas's dark mob past, knew exactly what she was doing.

For more than an hour before the auction had started, women clad in sleek barely there dresses with plunging necklines had sipped free drinks as they mingled with men, sizing up the "merchandise," whose duty it was to make small—and seductive—talk.

Lex had failed abysmally.

He was not one for platitudes, let alone parties. And volunteering for a bachelor auction rated way down there along with…God knows what. He couldn't think of anything worse right at this moment. Those sixty-three minutes of *schmingling,* and yes, he'd counted every one of those minutes, had been pure torture. Lex was not one for high-maintenance women, either. Been there, done that, had the scars and divorce papers to show for it. If he ever married again, he swore it was going to be to a Stepford wife who understood his devotion to his job and charity work with at-risk kids.

The bidding out in the hall suddenly hit the $60,000 mark. The crowd of ladies exploded into raucous cheers, and the live band picked up the pace, ratcheting tension with a soft *boom, boom, boom* of drums. Lex tugged irritably to loosen his red tie.

His partner, Special Agent Rita Perez, had suggested red—to get the blood pumping, she'd chuckled. She told him the color was a good foil to the classic dark FBI suit and white shirt. He was going to kill Perez for this. She was the one who'd coerced him into it in the first place.

It's for a good cause, Duncan. All proceeds will go to the Nevada Orphans Fund. Think of how it will help your boys.

He adjusted his holster, his body heating under his jacket as the crowd thunderously applauded the top bidder who'd nabbed Mr. Investment Banker for an insane $62,500. Lex was up next, after the Clark County skydiving instructor standing beside him backstage.

Think of the Orphans Fund....

"You ever see so much cleavage in one place?" said Mr. Skydiver, eyes fixed on the shimmering crowd of women as he peered around the curtain. "Mostly pumas, I figure."

"Excuse me?"

"They're not all cougars over the age 45, check it out—" Mr. Skydiver edged the heavy curtain back. "See? Hot pumas, single or divorced females between the ages of 30 to 40, all with serious cash to blow. Best way to meet a prospective date if you ask me." He jutted his chin toward the audience. "Each one of those women out there has had her bank balance vetted—a marriage made in pure heaven."

Lex stared at him blankly. This guy thought he was going to find *commitment* here? "This is Vegas, buddy. Place of transience, slight of hand, trickery and sin."

"Ah, but magic happens in Vegas." Mr. Skydiver grinned, took a sharp swig from a small silver hip flask and offered the flask to Lex. "Dutch courage, in the name of Johnnie Walker?"

Lex shook his head.

Mr. Skydiver capped his flask. "Just ask any tourist," he said as he slipped the flask back into his pants pocket. "When that plane touches down at McCarran International, all rational thought goes clean out the window, and suddenly anything is possible. Yeah, Vegas will do that to you."

The guy had clearly gotten a little too intimate with Johnnie Walker. Lex made a mental note never to book a skydiving lesson with this dude, but he vaguely wished he had taken him up on the offer of a nip from the flask. The man looked enviably happy, and this was one time in his life Lex sure wouldn't mind numbing himself with a bit of false bravado. But before he could finish his thought, or change his mind and take up the flask, Mr. Skydiver was nudged abruptly forward by the bustling backstage coordinator taking his Johnnie Walker down the runway with him. And the next thing Lex knew, it was his turn.

"You're on, agent!" He was forced out from the protection of the curtain by the backstage boss.

His throat dried instantly.

Larger-than-life images of himself in various poses played out on a massive screen behind the emcee and the auctioneer. "Meet FBI Special Agent Lexington Duncan, girls!" Blinding stage spotlights swung his way.

Lex blinked into the glare. All he could see of the crowd was a dark blot stabbed by the occasional glitter of jewels and flash of sequins as women moved. He reached for his breast pocket and put on the sunglasses that Perez had insisted he bring.

"For the record," intoned the emcee. "Agent Duncan's weapon is disarmed. But who knows, he just might load his gun later for the right bidder." A murmur of excitement rippled through the women. Not quite the shrieks generated by Mr. Skydiver. Worry wormed into Lex as he took his first tentative steps down the runway. Maybe he was going to get lowballed. But the bids started instantly, flying fast and furious. *Oh geez.*

Heat prickled over his brow as he forced his legs toward the end of the ramp that jutted out into the sea of tables, a 007 theme tune mocking him. When he reached the end of the ramp, the music segued into a thumping sexy beast of a beat that thrummed up through his body from the soles of shined-up shoes making his heart constrict in time to the rhythm. His body grew hot. He yanked at his collar.

Oh, boy, was he ever going to kill Perez for getting him into this. He was going to get her right alongside with the mystery woman who'd organized this circus.

You don't have to do anything other than volunteer your time…yeah, well there was his pride on the line now.

He could just imagine the guys in the field office tomorrow morning. He shoved his shades higher onto his face with a scowl he made no attempt to hide. Patience he had in buckets— on a job. Not now. Now he'd lost every last ounce and wanted to get this the hell over.

Irritability powered his body movements as he strutted forward with the classic command presence of a cop. He got to the end of the ramp, flipped open his jacket, showing his holster and weapon.

The ladies went wild.

"Want to see Special Agent Lexington Duncan load that pistol, ladies? You've got to make those numbers real arresting in order to be taken down to the station, girls. Maybe he'll pat you down, or frisk you…"

Bids rose—higher, hotter, faster.

Lex stalked back up to the top of the runway, getting more and more steamed. He took off his jacket, draped it over the emcee's podium. It was his little intrusion into her space, a psychological ploy. Another wave of hoots and hollers burst from the crowd at this apparent audacity. Women began to leave their tables and line the runway, cheeks flushed, eyes bright, music loud. Their hands were waving with cash, trying to reach up to stuff it into his pants.

A strange sort of energy caught him. This was what crowd hysteria did to one, he thought, loosening his red tie, unbuttoning his white shirt, knowing his muscles were getting amped from the adrenaline and…well, yeah, the attention. He was male after all. Every man had his pride. And libido. Be damned if Lex's competitive edge didn't stab suddenly into his chest. Hell, if he was on the stage now, he might as well win, right? Why not get the top bid from that teeming excited mass of over a thousand women with more cash to burn than they knew what to do with.

For the orphans, Lex. Think of your boys. A small grin of satisfaction settled over his mouth. If "his boys" could see him now. He'd better do them proud. Yeah, he'd get his money's worth out of these pumas.

He slowed his swagger, put some muscle into it as he stripped off his shirt, tossed it to the crowd. His body was ripped and tanned—honed to peak perfection from daily training workouts, his twice-weekly coaching sessions with his kids under the hot desert sun, his eyes and reflexes keen from hours at the range. Under that conservative buttoned-up FBI exterior lurked a very different Lex Duncan, and it showed—in the exuberant reaction from the crowd.

"Take it all off! Take it all off! Take it all off!"

The chant rose in crescendo, and the live musicians, adept at playing to their audience, worked the energy. Lex thrust even more swagger into his walk, tightening his jaw, squaring his shoulders aggressively. Under the glaring spotlights his tanned skin began to glisten. Paddles continued to shoot up around the hall, bids going alarmingly high with one suddenly hitting an all-time record.

"*Ninety thousand dollars!* We have ninety thousand from the bidder in silver at the back of the hall. Going once…" The gavel was raised dramatically, poised to slam down with flourish. Lex squinted into the far recesses of the vast Ruby Room, trying to see who was prepared to plunk down such a serious chunk of change for a date with him, but the chandeliers had been dimmed and the spotlights blinded him.

"Wait! We now have…ninety-five thousand from the lady in red at the table in front!"

His heart beat faster, he strutted harder. The music went louder. Yeah. He was going to nail it—a top bid. Walk away from this with ego intact.

"Going once…going twice…" Called the auctioneer. "Oh, we have one hundred thousand! Again from the bidder in silver at the rear."

The atmosphere shifted suddenly, and a hot hush of tension pressed down over the crowd. The music all but stopped, just whispering kettle drums.

The auctioneer's voice took a quiet edge. "We have a bid of one hundred thousand dollars, ladies. Going once. Going twice…"

Adrenaline quickened through Lex as he tried again to squint beyond the glare of the spotlights. This was insane. Then again, this was Vegas. Where people believed that everything had a price, any dream could be bought. Anything could happen. Maybe Mr. Skydiver was right after all. A small ripple of hot pleasure coursed through him. Someone wanted him bad, and that was good, because this entire event, this bidding war over him right now was going to buy some real programs for his "kids." Besides, how bad could one date get anyway?

* * *

It was Jenna Jayne Rothchild's turn to get steamed. Someone at the back of the room was giving her one hell of a run for her money, and she had zero intention of losing Special Agent Lex Duncan to *anyone.* This whole damn extravagant event had been created solely so she could nab him.

"Who the hell *is* that back there?" she whispered angrily through her teeth, eyes remaining fixed on the auctioneer.

"Mercedes Epstein," said Cassie Mills excitedly. "And…oh, my God, Jenna, she's wearing Balduccio. A full-length silver Balduccio gown. It's like…oh God, it's stunning. Even at *her* age."

Jenna, Vegas event planner extraordinaire and organizer of the Bachelor Auction for Orphans, shot a hard, fast look to the back of the massive ballroom. The chandeliers had been dimmed over the crowd of over a thousand women—each one of them vetted and personally invited by Jenna because they had the wherewithal to plunk down substantial amounts of cash. But even in the darkness, Jenna could make out the shimmering silver-white chignon belonging to the gracious head of 62-year-old Mercedes Epstein. Diamonds glittered around the neck of the Vegas matriarch, and her gown was a silvery-lilac, like platinum. Like moonlight. The woman seemed to glow spectrally in the dark as if she possessed a mysterious inner phosphorescence.

"Crap," Jenna hissed, getting hot in her own low-cut designer gown. "What in hell does she want?"

"Your FBI agent, *obviously,*" Cassie said with her dimpled grin.

"I didn't send her an invite!"

"Is there any lady out there prepared to up the ante to one hundred five thousand dollars for a night of her design with Special Agent Lexington Duncan at her side, for her protection?"

Jenna shot her paddle up aggressively.

She didn't like to lose. Not ever. Especially not to Mercedes

Epstein. It was a female pride thing. Vegas may be chocked to the gills with transients and tourists, but Sin City still had it's hierarchy among the high-end Strip "locals." Mercedes, known for her charity largesse, especially when it came to child-related charities, was married to Frank Epstein, one of the most powerful men in Vegas—no, make that Nevada. No make that one of the most influential men in the United States. He was worth billions on Wall Street and had funded the campaigns of many a senator, local sheriff and Vegas city councilor.

A small fist of cold tension curled through Jenna's stomach as she clutched her paddle. Frank Epstein also had a long-standing rivalry with her dad, Harold Rothchild. Mercedes could outbid her anyday—and might just do it to annoy one of the Rothchild clan. But for whatever reason the matriarch was here, Jenna was *so* not losing to the woman.

This was *her* show.

"I don't give a damn what she's wearing," Jenna ground out through her teeth. "Or how much she has in her bank account. She can't have him. He's mine. He's the whole bloody point I organized this auction."

"One hundred ten thousand, going once to the lady in silver at the back…"

Again Jenna shot her paddle up, her heart beating faster.

"We now have one hundred twenty thousand from the young lady in red at the front…and oh, wait, was that a slight twitch of the paddle from the mystery bidder's assistant at the back of the room? Yes…yes…a twitch from the bidder in silver's assistant at the back. We now have a new bid of one hundred twenty-five thousand big cool ones, people. From our mystery lady at the rear."

There was a collective intake of breath. A kinetic energy began to pulse through the hall. The antique Egyptian fans turned slowly overhead, and the kettle drums started rolling softly. The FBI agent on stage inhaled deeply, and it expanded his chest.

A hot rush of adrenaline coursed through Jenna at the sight of him, and suddenly she wanted more than just to win him for Daddy's sake. She wanted him for her own sake. Getting close to Lex Duncan had, however, been her father's idea—his request, in fact.

Harold Rothchild had asked Jenna to try and seduce information out of the agent after he'd gotten wind that Lex Duncan was now the lead investigator in his daughter Candace's homicide case. The FBI had also seized an infamous Rothchild family heirloom—the legendary Tears of the Quetzal—a chameleon diamond worth millions that had been taken from Candace's finger the night of her murder—a rock Candace herself had appropriated from Daddy's safe and waved around inappropriately and, apparently, at the expense of her life.

A rock rumored to be cursed with an old Mayan legend.

Supposedly, in the right hands, The Tears of the Quetzal would bring great love to whoever held the ring, even momentarily. But in the wrong hands, grave misfortune would be sure to follow.

Jenna thought the legend was a bunch of hooey. Then again, Candace *had* died because of it. And after Jenna's attorney cousin, Conner, had failed to retrieve the infamous diamond, her father, clearly obsessed with the stone, now wanted it back at any cost. He'd asked Jenna to help find a way. He'd asked her to try and seduce the FBI agent into telling her where The Tears of the Quetzal was now being kept. And her casino mogul father had been uncharacteristically edgy and insistent in doing so. He hadn't even mentioned the plan to Conner for fear Conner might tip the agent who'd become something of a friend. Whatever— Jenna was happy to oblige her dad. She liked to make him happy.

Besides, she could pretty much seduce a monk. She didn't think twisting the buttoned-up, übercool FBI agent around her pinky finger would pose much problem at all.

She'd started by staging a little covert investigation of her own, and she'd learned that Lex Duncan was a keen supporter of the Nevada Orphans Fund. He volunteered for the organization twice a week, coaching at-risk teenage boys. It was clearly a charity Lex Duncan held close to his heart, so she'd come up with the idea a Bachelor Auction for Orphans as the best way to get her hands on him.

Her best friend, Cassie Mills, had then been co-opted into coercing Lex's partner, Special Agent Rita Perez, into twisting the reticent agent's considerably muscled arm. It was the perfect plan—Cassie was a student at Rita's martial arts class at the club, so she already had an in with Lex's partner.

Besides, organizing the event was fun. Parties, each with more bling and glitz than the next, were Jenna's forte, her way of escaping reality, her way of running from the dark questions surrounding her sister's murder.

She wasn't good at the dark stuff—she was good at escaping. Survival, Vegas-style.

Jenna inhaled deeply and got to her feet. Whispers rustled through the crowd like wind bending the tips of dry grass.

The 25-year-old Vegas casino princess—heiress to considerable Rothchild fortune, and daddy's girl—was making it clear she intended to lock horns with the grande doyenne of the casino empire. Despite the fact Mercedes was married to Frank Epstein, the grizzled old lion king of the Strip, Jenna wasn't going to be intimidated by the Vegas matriarch's pedigree. And the battle lines were drawn over the federal agent standing on the stage, his half naked, bronzed and ripped body gleaming under the spotlights.

Camera flashes popped everywhere, reporters smelling tomorrow's headlines. The kettle drums rolled softly, winding tension tighter.

"One hundred fifty thousand," Jenna called out coolly. The Ruby Room fell so silent one could hear a pin drop.

Mercedes tipped her coiffed head almost imperceptibly to the man seated beside her—a massive personal assistant-cum-bodyguard in a designer suit who then flipped her paddle silently for her, his pockmarked features unmoving.

"We have one hundred seventy-five thousand dollars for the Nevada Orphans Fund!" The auctioneer pointed to the back. "Going to our mystery lady in silver and her assistant at the rear."

Heads swiveled again, eyes blinking into the darkness.

The lighting technicians scrambled to spin a spotlight toward the back of the room in an effort to illuminate the holder of the big purse. But the beam didn't reach. One of the techs hurriedly began to remount the light.

Jenna swallowed. Daddy was just going to have to foot the bill on this one. "One eighty," she called out, squaring her shoulders, smiling seductively, telegraphing outward calm and control—fully aware of the camera lenses on her and her photogenic quality.

"We now have one eighty," echoed the auctioneer.

Camera flashes popped, making the shimmering zircon crystal beads on her dress glitter like an electric waterfall. Silence pushed down heavier onto the room. The fans circled slowly overhead. Jenna swallowed past the tension in her throat, waiting.

"And…yes, yes, we have one ninety! From the back!"

Jenna cursed violently under her breath, flicked her paddle, smiling sweetly. She didn't look around, wouldn't give her rival the pleasure. She was posing now, for the cameras, out to win. On all counts.

But her opponent remained steadfast and countered instantly.

"One ninety-five, to the back."

Her mind raced, doing the math, second-guessing her father's reaction. He was already on the hook for the organization of the event, never mind her personal bid.

"Going once. Going…" The auctioneer raised the gavel

theatrically. Everyone seemed to lean forward in collective anticipation.

"Two hundred fifty thousand," Jenna said, voice clear as a bell.

Silence expanded, stretched, vibrated and shimmered like a taut invisible thing in the room.

"We have two hundred fifty thousand dollars, going once… going twice…"

The tech finally managed to remount the spotlight, and he swung it abruptly around, forcing white light into the dim back reaches of the Ruby Room, illuminating the Vegas matriarch in her full glory. She rose majestically to her feet. Tall and elegant.

Then with a gracious tip of her head, Mercedes deferred to Jenna and touched her assistant's broad shoulder. At the matriarch's signal her bodyguard rose and escorted his charge toward the grand gilt-engraved doors. He held them open for Mercedes, and she seemed to float from the room. The doors swung slowly, silently shut.

"*Sold!* To the lady in red." The gavel hit the block, and the crowd erupted, music exploded and Jenna's heart thudded wildly. "Special Agent Lexington Duncan fetches a record winning bid for the night, ladies. Please come up and claim your man, 159," the auctioneer said, referring to the number on Jenna's paddle.

"Damn, that was close," she whispered into Cassie's ear as she bent down and took a deep gulp of champagne from her glass. She then pressed her palms down on her hips, trying to remove the dampness and straighten out her nerves as she walked up to the stage. Agent Duncan stood shirtless, waiting to see the lady in the red dress who'd bought his pleasure. He removed his shades as she neared.

Jenna reached her hand up to him, and he clasped it. His grip was hard, rough, all power as he jumped down from the stage, landing beside her with a thud. Jenna's heart did a crazy little squeeze that made her catch her breath. Must be the adrenaline, she thought. But when she looked up into his moss-green eyes she knew it was more. Lots more. He raised her hand slowly to his lips and kissed the backs of her fingers lightly. "Touché," he whispered. "I'm yours for a night." Heat arced along her arm and stabbed into her heart like a jolt of pure electric current. She felt as if she'd just been sucker punched. One look and FBI Agent Lex Duncan had rendered Jenna Jayne Rothchild utterly—and uncharacteristically—speechless.

Cameras flashed blindingly, adding to her strange and sudden sense of confusion.

He bent down, mouth near her ear. "Just name the time and place for our date, and then I can get the hell out of here," he growled.

A smile curled slowly over her mouth. "Why, but you sound pissed, Agent Duncan. Are you unhappy with your date?"

"Lex," he said. "And it's not you—this is not my thing."

"Jenna," she said softly. "Jenna Jayne Rothchild."

He stiffened, recognition suddenly hitting him square between the eyes. He swore viciously under his breath.

"What's the matter? You have something against the Rothchilds as well as bachelor auctions?"

Hell yeah!

He'd just been "bought" by the heiress of the family he was investigating in connection with murder—a professional conflict of interest that could blow the whole damn case. He was instantly furious. He had to extricate himself ASAP.

"Look," he said hastily. "There's been one huge mistake. I need to bow out—"

"Oh, but you can't, Agent Duncan," she crooned. "I've just paid two hundred fifty thousand dollars for the pleasure of your company. You signed an agreement."

"This is a conflict of interest, Ms. Rothchild. I'm handling the investigation into your sister's homicide. And you know it."

She placed her cool, smooth hand on his amped forearm. "Do you want the Nevada Orphans Fund to be a quarter of a million poorer than it is right now?" she asked with a soft and flirtatious smile, her big dark eyes twinkling. "That money could be targeted specifically to your at-risk coaching program—the one you volunteer for two days a week."

She knew. Damn her. She knew enough about him to…a dark thought suddenly hit Lex. Jenna Jayne Rothchild was the events planner at the Grand Hotel and Casino, her father's largest Strip operation. She was renowned for her parties, each one more extravagant than the next.

"Was it you who organized this auction event, Ms. Rothchild?"

"Jenna," she reminded him, smiling sweetly. "And yes. It went rather well, don't you think? We must have raised close on—"

"You set me up."

"And why would I do that?"

To compromise my investigation, to send my case down the legal tubes if it ever reached court. Hell alone knew. Whatever her motive was, Lex was going to find out. Sexy little Jenna Jayne Rothchild had just made herself a key person of interest in his homicide investigation. He removed a card from his back pocket, slapped it onto the white damask linen that covered her table. "Call me when you've decided whether you can afford the donation—*without* the date. Because the deal is off."

"But—"

"Sorry," he snapped. "Can't mix business with…" He hesitated as she moved her sexy body closer to his amped one.

"You were going to say…pleasure?"

He felt heat. Swallowed.

"Because it sure wasn't business that I had in mind, Agent Duncan."

His throat began to thicken, and his brain headed south. "Sorry, no can do." But be damned if right at this insane moment

Lex was suddenly feeling it was *all* he wanted to do. This woman, up close, was pure bewitchment. He had to get out of her aura, suck in a dose of desert air, figure out what the hell to do about this stunt she'd pulled. He turned to go, just as the dance music was heating up and lights began to pulse over the floor.

"Wait." She grasped his arm. "At least give me this one dance?"

Lex stilled at the sensation of her hand on his bare arm, cognizant of the fact that he was still naked from the waist up. Her hand moved a little higher, and his stomach tightened sharply. He turned, slowly, and looked down into her deep liquid-brown eyes. *Mistake.*

Because suddenly he couldn't seem to pull away. "It's…nearly midnight," he managed, his voice thick. He tried to tell himself it was the excitement, the adrenaline pounding through his system. But it wasn't. It was her. She was doing this to him.

She laughed. "What? You worried your SUV will turn into a pumpkin?" she said naughtily with a little pout on her red lips, and he knew he was going to be toast if he didn't move. Real soon.

"I…have to report to work early tomorrow."

"Is it always about the job for you, Lex?"

He studied her brown eyes, drowning in them for a long moment. "Pretty much."

And his orphans. That was his life right now. That was the way he liked it.

Her eyes flickered, a mischievous glint in them. "We'll have to do something about that, then."

Oh, boy. On impulse he snagged a tequila from a passing tray, swigged it back, felt the oily burn through his chest. Another mistake. It seemed to shoot straight to his groin. Making him hotter, not to mention hard.

She moved her curvaceous body closer, almost pressing up against him. He could smell her fragrance, her warmth. The lights dimmed. Colored spotlights played over the dance floor, the crystal in the chandeliers shimmering in dazzling small pinprick shards of light. A low primal beat began to swallow the dance floor.

"Come," she whispered against his cheek. He felt her hand sliding down his arm, her fingers gently encircling his wrist. He could feel the warm swell of her breast against his bare torso, the soft champagne breath from her lips against his face, and she lured him, as if manacled, drawing him onto the dance floor. "Just one dance," she said. "Then I'll let you know where to pick me up tomorrow night."

Lex glanced desperately at the massive art deco clock on the wall. The luminous hands showed three minutes to midnight—the average length of a song. He vowed he'd be outta here within those minutes. Then he'd find a way to weasel out of the date. He was convinced she'd set him up. Because what were the odds of this being a coincidence? She'd have to have been living under a rock not to know he was the lead agent on her sister's homicide case. And under a rock was the last place this casino princess would be.

Then again, as Mr. Skydiver had pointed out, this was Vegas. Weird stuff—magic—really did happen. A gambler could bet a single quarter and pull a slot machine handle, and it would spew out one million dollars. Another could plunk down his life savings and lose his entire fortune with the simple flick of a card.

Luck. Fate. Chance. The only sure thing about Las Vegas was that nothing was sure, nothing predetermined. No one ever knew what could happen next.

It's what made Sin City so exciting.

So dangerous.

Jenna placed her hands on his hips, guiding him to the rhythm of the beat, and Lex's brain went blank. His blood began to thump in time with the music. And before he knew it, the trademark Ruby Room clock began to chime. Midnight.

Music halted momentarily for effect, twirly strips of silver confetti shimmering down like crystal rain as the lights strobed white. Like silver, like money. Like magic. The Vegas sleight-of-hand. And Lex knew, on some level, he'd been witched, by a pair of big brown eyes and a goddess body in a shimmering red dress, and it had happened somewhere in those three minutes before the stroke of midnight.

In panic he snagged another shot of tequila, knocked it back, thinking of Dutch courage and skydiving. Because he sure was free-falling right now, out of control, and gaining speed each time Jenna batted those big browns and arched against him.

Chapter 2

The DJ amped the music, and the base pulsed deeper. Bodies gyrated, red strobes flashing off glass in the chandeliers, off the red crystals on Jenna's dress, and the tequila began to work on Lex's brain, along with his libido.

Truth was, the more Lex looked at her, the more bedazzled he was by Jenna Rothchild. She had the kind of looks that really did it for him—rich chestnut hair that fell in lustrous waves to well below her creamy shoulder blades. Full mouth, painted blood-red, high cheekbones that gave her an air of experienced sophistication—the kind that made a man forget about her youth—and a body worth every bit of wattage in Sin City. *That* made a man hot.

It wasn't easy to stand out in a place like Vegas—a town of lean, leggy showgirls with spotlight smiles—but this woman did. She was also big money and high maintenance, and for all those reasons, Lex wanted to avoid her like the plague. Never mind a conflict of interest. Jenna Jayne Rothchild was plain dangerous to him personally as well as professionally.

But as he was about to pull back and extricate himself while he still could, she leaned up and murmured against his cheek. "You feel a little stiff, agent."

Oh yeah, and she was going to find out just how stiff if she pressed her body any closer to his pelvis. The music wasn't the only thing hot and pulsing right now.

She used her hands to guide his body in time to the retro beat. "Come on, loosen up a little, move with me, agent. Or are you always wound this tight?"

Unsmiling, he allowed her to move his hips to the primal tempo of the music and be damned if all he could think about was getting her into bed, and moving with her like a real man, naked between the sheets, the way nature intended. It made his head thicker, it made his vision narrow, it made perspiration begin to gleam over his bare chest.

Lex tried to stay in focus, thinking he should never have downed those shots, because he was not feeling himself. Instead, he found himself fixated on her cleavage, the way the neckline of her dress plunged so low that the sparkling fabric seemingly just floated atop her breasts. He had no idea how it stayed there. And he found himself *waiting* for it to slip, lust winding so tight inside him he thought he'd bust. Then as she moved, the diamond teardrop pendant nestled between her smooth breasts at the end of a gold chain, winked at him.

And the thought of the big diamond rock in FBI lockdown suddenly slammed into him. The Tears of the Quetzal. The case he was working.

The homicide.

His job.

He leaned down to tell Jenna he was leaving, but she placed two fingers over his lips and shook her beautiful head. "No," she mouthed over the music. Then she leaned up again, whispering in his ear. "Don't think. Just dance with me. Find my rhythm." Her voice reverberated softly against his skin, breath warm in his ear as she swayed seductively against him. He felt her hands slide up the sides of his naked torso, lingering over ridges of muscle, exploring his body inch by inch as she moved. A shaft of heat shot clean to his groin and Lex's breath strangled in his chest. For some reason, Harold Rothchild's youngest daughter was really working him.

She was trapping him with her magic, and she knew it. And his lust was beginning to feed on itself like a forest fire. Lex was going to have one hell of a time trying to put this carnal genie that had been awakened back into its little bottle.

She moved her mouth toward his, brushing her red lips over his, allowing the barest tip of her tongue to enter his mouth and touch the inner seam of his top lip.

Lex's world swirled darkly. He opened his mouth, unable to stop himself from tasting her.

And suddenly, another camera flashed, capturing the moment.

Lex blinked, shocked instantly back to reality. He cursed viciously.

He could just see the headlines tomorrow: *Half-Naked FBI Agent in Charge of High-Profile Vegas Homicide Locks Lips on the Dance Floor with Victim's Younger Sister.*

He was toast.

He had to get the hell out of here—and fast.

Lex *lived* for his job. The Bureau, his "kids," the old Washoe County sheriff who'd pulled him back from the edge when he was being bounced from one foster home to the other—*those* things were his family. And he had no intention of blowing it all over a woman.

Especially *this* woman.

He grabbed her wrist firmly, his jaw tense as he escorted her brusquely toward the doors. The teeming, dancing crowd of bodies parting in front of him like the Red Sea. He ushered her out into the hall where it was quieter.

The doors shut sullenly behind them.

"You set me up, Jenna. Why?" he demanded. "Did you do this to compromise the case? What's in it for *you?*" The direct approach, all business, was the only way for Lex to steer himself clear of his own libido right now.

She blinked those impossibly big, sparkling eyes. "I had no idea you were on the case, Lex."

"You'd have to be living under a rock not to know!"

"I don't follow all that—" she waved her hand dismissively "—technical stuff."

He cupped her jaw, lifted it up. "Don't give me the bimbo spiel, Ms. Rothchild. I suspect you have more intellect stashed in your pretty little head than Mr. Investment Banker with the rose wilting in his teeth back there. What game are you playing? What're you trying to achieve here? If you're trying to mess with this case because you have something to hide, I promise you now, I *will* find it."

She swallowed, pupils darkening reflexively. Heat ribboned through him.

"Look," he said, his voice coming out an octave lower. "It's up to you what you do with that quarter million, but I'm outta here."

"You still owe me a date, Lex."

"I owe you nothing, Jenna."

"If you want that money to go to charity," she said with a defiant tilt of her head, "you'll spend a few hours with me."

He glared at her. "An ultimatum? Oh, that's rich."

"We had a deal."

"What we have, Jenna, is a conflict of interest."

"Not to my mind. And if you don't play, agent, I don't give."

She made a moue, and all he could think about was kissing those full, pouty red lips of hers.

Lex swallowed against the dryness in his throat. And before reengaging his brain, the words came out of his mouth. "One date. That's it. The money goes to my kids. Then this is done. Over. *Capiche?*"

"What ever made you think I wanted—" her eyes teased slowly over his bare chest "—anything more?" she whispered. "I did this purely for charity, Lex."

He muttered something unholy under his breath. Then spun, and stalked off toward the hotel lobby.

Jenna watched him go, admiring the view. His dark-blond hair glinted under the pinprick lights, and his neck was taut. The power in his shoulders transferred with each stride down the corded muscles of his broad back into the waistband of his tailored pants—pants that had been expertly cut to accommodate the rock-hard thighs she'd felt against her body while dancing. And suddenly, this really wasn't about Daddy and the diamond at all. Not even remotely. This was about Jenna. What *she* wanted…and she wanted him.

Except he appeared immune to her charms. And her money.

Lex Duncan had just tossed down the gauntlet, because Jenna never failed, *especially* when it came to men. She always got what she wanted from a guy, and this one was making her determined to prove her skill.

And Jenna had learned from early childhood how to manipulate the males in her life, starting with her dad.

Her mother, June Smith Rothchild, had died while giving birth to Jenna, and she'd always felt that others in her family, including her father, saw her as somehow responsible for June's death. And when Jenna and her older twin sisters—Candace and Natalie—had fought, Candace would get nasty and "remind" Jenna she "killed their mom." These attacks had made

Jenna feel like an outsider in her own family. Not to mention guilty. She'd become a sensitive and lonely child with a driving need to be loved, to please and to be liked.

And as she got older, Jenna sometimes caught her dad watching her in a certain way. It was at those times that Jenna knew she was reminding him of the wife he truly loved and missed. And although Jenna knew her father totally adored her, his feelings about his youngest daughter were complex. On occasion, especially after a few nighttime single malts, Harold would lash out irrationally at Jenna because she reminded him so painfully of June.

Those moments caused Jenna extreme hurt, and it became her goal to do anything she could to keep in her daddy's good graces. To be liked by him, to be his favorite daughter. He was her rock. Her defense against the twins, against the nasty friends at school, and she'd found that flattery worked. It was the beginning of where Jenna learned to charm males, with very real results. She'd come to realize she could get whatever she needed this way.

It was the same in high school. Because of her seductive beauty Jenna was automatically labeled as promiscuous. So, to stay "cool" and "liked" she pretended to be "bad," wore the sexy clothes, hung out with the in crowd. And she always managed to hide her giving heart, her sharp intelligence and her genuine sensitivity. No one had ever really gotten to know the real Jenna Rothchild.

And Jenna started to become the person she had so carefully fashioned. Because of this, she continued to attract the wrong sort of men post school, and she continued to escape with parties. Throwing fabulous events became her forte, her way to escape uncomfortable reality, to be the center of attraction— to be *liked*. And she was so good at the parties it grew into a business, her dad eventually hiring her as a key event planner for his major Strip casino—the Grand Hotel and Casino.

But deep down, something was missing. A pit was forming in Jenna's gut—a longing for a sense of worth, something real. Some value and relevance in the scope of the world. And she'd begun to harbor secret fears that maybe she really had no personality after all. Then with Candace's murder, the inner Jenna really began stirring, asking questions about what life and money were really all about when it couldn't buy the kind of happiness her poor beleaguered sister seemed to have been yearning for.

Her dad approaching her for help in Candace's case was a way to wrest some control of it all. To do *something*.

And now there was this bonus—Special Agent Lexington Duncan.

He was pure eye candy. She wanted him and was stunned he'd been able to resist her, especially after she'd coughed up a cool quarter million for his pet charity.

Damn cool solid hunk of granite.

It made her all the more determined and just a little bit vulnerable.

She pushed a wave of hair back from her face, watching him exit the hotel, shirtless. And she allowed amusement to whisper over her lips. Poor devil. He'd thrown his shirt to the crowd of bidding women, and now he was apparently too proud to go back inside to look for something to wear. The FBI agent was left with no choice but to go home half-naked.

Her smile deepened into a grin.

She'd get him.

She'd seal the seduction tomorrow, on their date.

This was just phase one, she told herself. She'd done her reconnaissance, and gotten him here—playing it smart, staging the event away from the Grand Hotel and Casino and keeping her own name off the event ticket.

Enlisting Cassie to approach Lex's partner, Rita Perez, at the gym where Rita gave martial arts classes two evenings a week had been the coup de grâce.

Yeah, the date itself would be phase two. And once she was done there, he'd be pure, warm putty in her hands. And that thought sent a hot little tingling zing of anticipation through her belly. She exhaled, pressing her hand against her stomach as she watched the glass revolving door spew him out into the hot desert night. The valet rushed over to him, called for his car.

As Lex passed by on the other side of the big glass windows making his way toward his black SUV he glanced up, caught her watching and scowled.

She smiled sweetly and gave a little wave.

Then she spun on her four-inch heels and sashayed back toward the pulsing Ruby Room. But as she pulled open the doors, she bumped into Cassie coming out.

"Uh-oh," Cassie said the minute she saw her friend. "You have that look."

"What look?"

Cassie glanced over Jenna's shoulder, saw the shirtless cop through the windows getting into his SUV. "Oh, come on, Jenna. Why do you want *him* so bad, when you could have any one of the guys back there?"

Jenna didn't answer for a minute.

"Ah, wait, I get it." Cassie's disarming chuckle bubbled up from her chest. "It's because he's immune to the infamous Jenna Rothchild charm, is that it? He doesn't want *you*. Because he can see right through you, girlfriend."

Jenna laughed, making light of it while she said goodbye to her friend. But Cassie's words left a niggling coolness inside her. Maybe Cass was right.

Maybe Lex did see right through her. And he saw there was nothing inside. Nothing under the money and superficial glitz.

Jenna wasn't sure how to handle this idea. It made her feel

more than just a little bit vulnerable—it made her feel worthless. Maybe she was wrong. Maybe Lex Duncan had nailed the game advantage and she hadn't won after all.

Lex was greeted by a chorus of adult males making the yipping sounds of a small dog as he walked into the bullpen at the FBI's Las Vegas field office Friday, the next morning.

He glanced at Rita Perez. "What the hell is going on here?"

"She has one of those little purse pooches," Perez said as Lex removed his jacket.

"What are you talking about?"

Perez slapped a copy of the *Las Vegas Sun* on Lex's desk. "You and *it-girl*." She folded her arms across her chest, looking too damn smug for her own Latina good. Lex glanced down and saw the photo he knew he would. The one that showed him half-naked, gleaming with perspiration and kissing the Vegas heiress who was also the youngest sister of his homicide case victim.

He swore under his breath.

More yips taunted him.

"What's a *purse pooch* anyway?" he said, glaring at the press photo, growing hot under his collar.

"One of those little it-girl dogs, you know? The kind that cost several grand and fit right inside a designer purse. Look—" Perez flipped the paper open to page four, tapped the page annoyingly with her finger. "There. A file photo of your casino princess on a little shopping spree with her pooch and daddy's money, no doubt. Note—" said Perez, bending forward for emphasis "—that the purse matches Rothchild's outfit, as does that cute little bow in the dog's hair."

"What the hell kind of dog is that anyway…look at it's teeth. It's got an underbite like it's permanently mad at the world."

"Shih-Tzu," said Rita.

"Shih-t-*what?*"

Guffaws of laughter burst from the room, and more yipping came from the far corner of the bull pen.

"Shih-Tzu," corrected Perez. "It's Vietnamese."

"Chinese!" called an agent from across the room.

Another crescendo of yips rose through the office.

"Geez," Lex muttered, shuffling papers off his desk. "Bunch of losers."

"Agent Duncan!"

He glanced up sharply to see Harry Quinn, FBI Special Agent in Charge, standing at the rail up a level at the offices. He was holding a copy of the *Las Vegas Sun,* the big black headline sticking out over his thumb: "Record Two Million Raised for Nevada Orphans Fund."

"Can I see you in my office." It wasn't a question.

"Ooh, he's in the shih tzu doo-doo now," someone cooed in a loud stage whisper. More raucous laughter rolled through the bullpen. Lex swore softly as he made his way into Quinn's office.

Quinn slapped the paper down on his desk. The photo of Lex, topless, partying down with a person of interest in his homicide investigation mocked him from the polished surface. From the look in his boss's eyes, Lex was about to hear that he was off the case. Or worse.

He cleared his throat. "I can explain—"

Quinn raised his hand. "Let me see if I've got this straight," he snapped. "Jenna Rothchild paid a quarter of a million? To date *you* for a night?"

Lex ran his tongue over his teeth. "Yes, sir."

His boss suddenly threw back his head and laughed. Hard, really hard. He slumped down into his chair, wiping a tear from his eyes.

"Geez, Quinn, I'm not that much of a dog," Lex muttered. "Besides, I told her to forget it. Mistake. Conflict of interest. This—" he wagged his hand at the newspaper on Quinn's desk

"—will all blow over by tomorrow." Why did he not sound more convincing to himself?

His boss sat forward suddenly, eyes dead serious again. He had a way of switching back and forth, unnerving people. It kept his agents on their feet. "No." His black eyes bored into Lex. "No. This is not over. We use this. We use *her.*"

"Excuse me?"

"Play along."

Surprise rippled through Lex. He had zero intension of messing any further with Jenna for personal, never mind professional, reasons. "That's…ridiculous. It's a clear conflict of interest. It could pose a problem for the prosecution if they find a connection between me and Rothchild, especially if a defense attorney gets wind of—"

"Granted, yes, it's unorthodox." Quinn tapped his pen impatiently on his desk. "But *nothing* about this case to date has been orthodox. Consider it a covert operation, Duncan. A Rothchild infiltration." He leaned back in his chair as he spoke, and Lex detected a faint smirk of amusement on his superior's face.

"There's no way—"

"She's a tool, agent. She handed herself to us on a silver platter. *Use* that tool, leverage it to get to her father, to dig up information on that little trophy wife of his, on the dead sister, crack anyone or anything open, pry it loose. Play her game. One hundred percent. God knows we need some kind of break on this case."

"She set me up."

"So? Find out why."

"The media will—"

"I'll let the media know you're officially off the case. Unofficially, you're on it 24/7. We'll plug it as a covert op, and the legal stuff will be in the clear as long as you keep your hands off her."

"Look, I—"

His boss stood, making up in breadth what he lacked in Lex's height. "It's good to have you in the Vegas office, agent. I was more than happy to approve your request for transfer."

"Thank you, sir." That was a veiled threat if he ever saw one. Lex was no idiot. He'd put in for a post at this Las Vegas field office several times over the last couple of years, wanting to get out of Washington and back to the Reno-Vegas area for reasons of his own.

His application had been approved nine months ago, thanks in major part to Harry Quinn. And Lex had settled in fast, coaching troubled foster kids at football, volunteering for Nevada orphans-related charities. He'd landed himself a nice little house in one of the new subdivisions away from the hubbub of the Las Vegas Strip from where he could see the fire-red spring mountains. It was his springboard to the desert wilderness he'd always loved as a kid, yet not too far from the sort of pulse he'd grown up with in Reno. In many ways, Lex felt he'd come right home to Sin City. His mother had a past here, and it was here he'd come looking for answers. Lex was finally in a position to put everything into finding the man who had killed his mother.

He had no intention of being eased out now. If keeping this posting meant tangling with Jenna Rothchild, he'd have to bite the bullet and try to keep his libido in check. In spite of what moves she pulled on him.

Damn—he was between a rock and a hard place. He could already hear the snickers out in the bullpen.

He blew out a chestful of air as Quinn showed him out the office door. "And keep me briefed, Duncan. Let me know if you need anything. Perez remains your backup on this."

Perez was the one who got me into this.

He saw her smiling up at him as he neared his desk. "I wanted to kill you last night," he muttered as he approached.

She grinned, teeth bright-white against her dusky skin. "And now?"

"Even more so. You better watch your back, Perez."

She chuckled. "I'll be too busy watching yours. Just make sure you keep your shirt on this time, will you?"

He grunted as he took a seat at his desk.

"Did you actually read that article, Duncan?" she called over to him.

"You got any work to do there, Perez?"

"No, seriously, did you see who the hot competition was for your bod? Who the mystery bidder was that gave our little it-girl a run for her daddy's money?"

"Who?" He fussed with moving papers across his desk, feigning disinterest.

"Mercedes Epstein."

He went stone still then turned slowly to look at Perez.

"*Si, amigo,* that's right," she said, getting up and sauntering over to his desk to him with that devil-can-do look in her Latina eyes. "Wife of *the* Frank Epstein, who's currently under investigation with the FBI financial crimes unit in New York. Some junk bond scam, apparently."

Mercedes had bid on him? The wife of the man who had once employed his mother in his Vegas casino as a croupier? The man who'd fired Sara Duncan when she fell pregnant with him, necessitating her move to Reno, to start a new life. Just him and her.

"Interesting, huh?"

It was plain freaking weird. "Mmm," he said, opening a file, but his pulse had quickened.

"So, what d'you think the grand Vegas matriarch wanted with you? You think she pushed up the bidding just to get up Jenna's whatoot?"

He glanced up sharply. "Tell you what, Perez. Why don't

you and me go for a little drive and check out that new shooting range? And while we're there you can tell me how and why you signed me up for that bachelor auction while I try not to shoot you. Because I'm thinking it was *you* who set me up, not the Rothchild heiress."

"Sure," she shrugged. "We can go shoot. From that photo it looks like you could let off a few."

He grabbed his jacket angrily, took her elbow. "For starters," he growled as he led her out the door, "who approached you about the auction?"

"Cassie Mills. She takes a class at the club where I teach martial arts."

"She Jenna's friend?"

"How the hell would I know?"

Jenna was feeling an inescapable buzz. Being attracted to a man she was going to see that night was like a drug to her system, a welcome relief from all the sadness that had beset the Rothchild mansion since Candace's horrible death. "Good morning, Dad," Jenna said, as she bent down to kiss her father on the cheek. She set a bowl of doggie kibble down for Napoleon, poured coffee from the silver jug Mrs. Carrick, their cook, had left on the patio breakfast table and took a seat with a view of the pool.

The surface shimmered with refracted morning sunlight as Jones, their groundskeeper, cleaned the pool filter. A soft, hot desert breeze ruffled the tops of the garden palms. It was late June, Vegas peaking into summer, and today was going to be a scorcher.

"So?" Harold said over the top of his paper and his reading glasses, his Paul Newman-blue eyes twinkling. "Two mil for the orphan fund? Not bad, sweetheart."

She grinned. "The FBI agent is not too bad either."

"When is your date?"

"Tonight. I just sent him a text message asking for his address and to say my limo will be waiting outside his house at 10 p.m."

"Rather late for dinner?"

She shrugged. "He said he had some kind of evening coaching session with his at-risk teens or something. Anyway, I told him I wanted white flowers and that the rest of the evening was my treat—" she stirred her coffee, chinked the spoon on the side, smiling "—and my surprise."

Jenna liked this time with her dad. He was a flamboyant casino mogul with movie-star good looks, a much-noted temper, a passion for perfection and a shrewd eye for business. He liked to get up real early each morning, do work in his home office and then kick back for a while over breakfast. It was his time to catch up with Jenna and the newspapers and to drink his coffee. After that he'd go down to the Grand Hotel and Casino, where he often worked well after midnight. He was a driven entrepreneur, and he wasn't a man who needed much sleep.

But he'd always made time for her, since she was a kid, and Jenna loved him for it. She'd do just about anything for her father. He remained the solid center of her rarefied Vegas life. Her BlackBerry beeped suddenly, and Jenna set down her coffee cup, checked the message. It was from Cassie. FBI agent Perez had apparently just paid her friend an "official" visit, and Cassie wanted to know what Jenna had gotten her into.

"You'll ask him about the ring, of course."

Frowning, her eyes flashed up. "Of course." She hesitated. "Dad—you've always said that The Tears of the Quetzal came from granddad's South American operations, but where exactly?"

"Ah, sweetheart, I'm not one hundred percent sure. All I know for certain is that your grandfather had the diamond set down there, but otherwise, all the paperwork seems to have been lost in an old fire at the South American office."

She studied him. If there's one thing Harold always was, it was sure. A teensy icicle of doubt formed. "What exactly do you want me to get out of Lex Duncan?"

He chuckled, removed his reading glasses, blue eyes sparking like the broken surface of the pool catching sun behind him. Yet there was a sharp edge that lurked behind his smile—an edge that appeared whenever Harold spoke about The Tears of the Quetzal. "Anything you can, sweetheart. You could make a monk drop his habit, Jenna, and I have no doubt you can work your charms on this man. I want some idea of the FBI's thought process in connection with the case. And of course I want my ring back. I want to know where they are holding it. In the wrong hands it—"

"I know the drill—in the wrong hands great misfortune is sure to follow. In the right hands it brings true love. You don't honestly believe that old Mayan nonsense, do you?"

He gave her an odd glance. "Just look what happened when that lunatic Thomas Smythe got a taste for it. He almost killed Conner's Vera, not to mention her sister Darla and brother Henry. Although the cops haven't officially named Smythe as a suspect in Silver's near-fatal scaffolding accident, I wouldn't put it past him. And God only knows who killed Candace. That damn ring is cursed, I tell you. I just want it out of circulation, back in the vault where it belongs before it causes any more damage."

A small shiver passed through Jenna as she thought of what had happened to Candace after she'd removed the rock from daddy's safe. Her sister had gone and gotten herself bludgeoned to death after wagging it around at a charity event the night before her murder. That ring had been the one thing taken from Candace's apartment by the killer, only to turn up in the purse of a single mother named Amanda Patterson while she was visiting Luke Montgomery's casino.

Having possession of that ring had close to gotten Amanda killed as well. And then Luke had stepped up and proposed to her, of *all* people.

The ring had subsequently been taken into Las Vegas Metropolitan Police Department custody, and a man named Thomas was later ID'd as the thief who impersonated a LVMPD officer and stole the ring from the evidence room. Conner had discovered the paste copy left in its place when he'd been sent to retrieve the ring from the police department. He'd then tracked The Quetzal to an exotic dancer and landed bang in the middle of an FBI investigation into a cross-state jewelry thieving ring. Which is how Conner ended up defending—and falling for—a stripper named Vera Mancuso who'd been implicated in the diamond theft by her roommate. The jewel thieves had, however, been caught and that case closed, but it was at that point that the LVMPD and FBI investigation into Candace's murder had intersected, and how the whole shebang—both the ring and murder—had landed up under FBI jurisdiction.

And now her dad wanted that ring back at all costs.

Jenna shook off an uneasy sensation, reached down and picked up Napoleon. She stroked him absently on her lap. She suddenly wasn't so crystal clear on what she was doing with the lead investigator on her sister's murder case.

Or why her father wanted her involved at all.

Lex returned to the FBI field office building after his coaching session that evening to pick up some reports. He wanted to go through the file on The Tears of the Quetzal again, check out the ring's trail. Somehow, that rock was central to everything—including Candace Rothchild's death. And now that Thomas Smythe—Darla St. Giles's boyfriend—had disappeared, Lex was back at square one.

It was late and most of the offices were empty and dark. Lex flipped on the neon overheads. One of the bulbs flickered as he made his way down the corridor to evidence lockup. He hesitated outside the door, a sense of coolness settling over his skin. Damn AC thermostat was on the fritz again, turning the place into a virtual meat locker. He unlocked the heavy door, creaked it open. He hadn't noticed the creak previously—must be the quietness in the building at this time of night.

Lex picked up the box containing the rock that had caused so much trouble and opened it. He took the ring between his thumb and forefinger, holding the massive stone up to the dim light, he swiveled it.

He was momentarily blinded by a flash of green, violet, then blue light. His pulse accelerated slightly. He'd never seen the rock in this light before. It was magical. He turned it more slowly in his fingers, the facets of light bouncing electrically as it moved. The Tears of the Quetzal. Even the name seemed sad. Somehow poignant. Yet beautiful at the same time. Seven carats of chameleon diamond. Set in gold.

The colors were dazzling. The strange luminous shafts of light emanating from the stone were like the ectoplasmic fingers of some ghost, reaching out to curl back and retreat suddenly as he moved the ring. The play of luminosity absorbed Lex's attention so fully, so totally, that he was no longer aware of any sound at all in the office, or the fact he was standing alone in near dark under the flickering blue lighting of the evidence room. A band of sensation tightened across his chest as an incredible thought shimmered into his mind.

What if the legend was true?

Natalie, the LVMPD cop—Jenna's sister and Candace's twin—had fallen in love while investigating the ring's disappearance. Then Amanda Patterson, whose purse it was found in, ended up marrying Luke Montgomery in a true Cinderella series of events. After which Silver Hesse Rothchild, a stepsister of Jenna's, had found true love with her bodyguard after a mere passing acquaintance with the ring. Even defense lawyer Conner Rothchild had fallen head over heels for Vera Mancuso, an exotic dancer, after he'd spotted her flashing the ring during a steamy striptease. Vera was probably the most inappropriate woman a man like Rothchild could possibly end up with.

Enduring love—it was one of the promises of The Tears of the Quetzal.

Given the odd series of romantic events in the preceding months one might actually be forgiven for thinking this ring held mysterious power, thought Lex, watching the light curl into itself in the stone, as if a sentient thing. Alive. Shimmering. All-knowing. He snorted softly, trying to brush aside the hypnotic power the thing seemed to be exerting over him.

Then he thought of Candace and the flip side to the supposed Mayan curse on this stone. And a cold chill rippled over his skin again as he stared at it, his heart beginning to beat even faster, a strange sensation beginning to settle through him. Lex couldn't say why or what possessed him but he suddenly pocketed the ring, leaving the box empty as he locked the evidence door.

Chapter 3

"So, what are you doing in Sin City, Lex?"

Lex regarded Jenna warily, his body language defensive as he sat across the table from her. His job tonight was to work Jenna Rothchild for whatever information he could. And then get out fast.

But things were already going sideways.

Jenna was clearly in the driver's seat. Having her limo pull up at his humble suburban driveway was no doubt a power play on her part. So was her "request" to be greeted with a bouquet of white flowers.

During the limo ride Jenna had plied him with top Scotch en route to one of the most opulent establishments in a city already renowned for excess. More cocktails awaited at the restaurant, which she'd reserved solely for the two of them—an octagonal, glassed-in affair that revolved slowly over the Vegas skyline. Candles shimmered in crystal holders on every table, a silvery sheet of water cascaded over a rock feature into a pool of lilies in the center of the room, while staff, dressed in black and white, stood discreetly in the shadows. And sitting at a baby grand, tinkling ivories for them alone, was a renowned singer from New Orleans with husky jazz vocals to rival the best of Nina Simone.

Lex would bet his last red casino chip that Jenna's choice of music was intentional. Somehow she'd known he loved jazz.

That meant she knew way too much about him.

"I hear you've been in town nine months now, Lex, and that you put in for the transfer to the Vegas field office from your post in Washington."

Definitely too much.

Jenna smiled the smile of a woman who knew exactly what wattage she generated. She was dressed in pure, virginal white and looked anything but virginal. Her blouse was low-cut, sheer. Her palazzo pants were silky. She wore them over impossibly high strappy gold sandals, and Lex had been unable to stop himself from fixating on the way the fabric had swished around her long legs when she walked. Or was that sashayed? Jenna didn't do anything ordinary like "walk."

In contrast to the white silk, her butter-smooth skin was tanned a soft biscuit-brown, and her limbs were taut—a woman with time for the pool and the gym. She looked vibrant, athletic, radiantly alive. And somehow sophisticated at the same time. Pure privileged casino princess. And way out of his league. Hell, she was out of his freaking hemisphere.

Her eyes glinted with some secret amusement as she waited for him to answer. Lex wondered if it was his obvious discomfort that she found so entertaining. "And you got this information from who?" he said guardedly.

She swiveled the stem of the crystal glass. "Let's just say I mounted a little covert investigation of my own." Her eyes slanted up. "I learned quite a few things about you, agent."

"Including the fact I like jazz?"

"Maybe." She smiled.

"Cassie Mills? Did she wheedle it out of my partner, Perez, at the gym?"

"Perhaps." She took a slow sip of champagne, eyes fixed on his with a directness that made him think of sex. "Is that why the feds paid Cassie a visit today?"

He leaned forward, irritation beginning to lance dangerously through the lust burning a hot and persistent coal into his gut. "How about we just cut to the chase, Jenna? Are you trying to compromise the investigation? Is that what the auction stunt was about?"

Maybe he'd just blown his chance at getting anything out of princess here, but he'd had his fill. Spending any more time with Jenna Rothchild was going to be real bad for his health. And quite possibly his job. Because no matter what Quinn had ordered, Lex could see himself taking the fall if this so-called "under the covers" operation—a farce if he ever saw one—went downhill. And because this murder and this Vegas family was so high-profile, FBI top brass would need to make an example of him. He could smell it all from a mile away.

And it stunk.

She cast her eyes down, tracing her fingertips slowly, seductively along the silver knife alongside her plate. Lex felt his body go hot.

"No, Lex," she said finally. "I did not set you up to mess with the investigation." She lifted her eyes. "I'll concede, though, that I did know you were the lead in the investigation, but when I glimpsed you at Natalie's wedding and saw your photo in the paper, I also knew you'd be the star of my bachelor auction, *if* I could get you. I also figured it would be a tough sell to get you to play because of your involvement with the case, so I kept my name out of it and sent Cassie to talk to Rita instead. We learned you had a thing for the Nevada Orphans Fund, so I swung the entire event around you. And then, when I saw you up on that stage, half-naked and getting all hot under your tie, well—" she paused, watching him intently "—I just had to have you for myself." She placed her cool hand over his. "Does that make you angry, Special Agent Duncan?"

Lex tried not to flush. Crap, he didn't even know where to look for a moment. She was flat out, shamelessly, seducing him. Or mocking him.

How far did she really want to go? He glanced down at her hand, her slender fingers splaying slowly over his, and perspiration prickled under his dress shirt. The idea he could have sex, tonight, with this intensely gorgeous young heiress—*if* he so chose—lodged hot and fast and sharp in his very male mind. And Lex knew he wasn't going to get the image out of his head any time soon. His gut turned molten, and his brain felt thick. Quinn's words crawled into his mind.

The legal stuff will be in the clear as long as you keep your hands off her.

Yeah, sex was the last thing he needed.

"Look, I don't know what game you're playing, Rothchild, but I'm not buying the fact you just felt like raising money for an arbitrary charity, for fun."

She made a moue. "You *are* angry." She feathered the back of his hand softly with her long red nails. "But you do look rather cute when you're worked up." Leaning forward, she lowered her voice to a whisper. "I knew there was a fire buried somewhere inside that buttoned-up suit of yours." She slipped her manicured nails gently between his fingers as she spoke.

Heat arrowed straight to his groin. "I don't like being played, Jenna," he said, his voice thick. "You know what I think? The real reason behind this whole auction gig is to have my case thrown out of court down the road, when Rothchild lawyers start pointing out I was having a relationship with the victim's sister. Maybe you want to see my career tank right along with the case, too?"

Her eyes flared.

He leaned forward. "And what *I* want, is to know why? What's in it for *you*, Jenna Rothchild? Is it because you're trying to hide some personal involvement in Candace's murder by obfuscating things like this? Because this is not some party trick, some amusing distraction for a bored young socialite. This is serious. This, Jenna, is life and death, because there's still a killer out there." He paused. "One who could very well strike again."

Her eyes flickered sharply, and a blush started to rise up her neck. Lex went for the gap. "Do you not want to find your sister's killer, Jenna? Do you not want a murderer punished?"

She withdrew her hand, glanced away for a moment. "I'm not trying to hide anything," she said very quietly. "Of course I want Candace's killer brought to justice."

Lex zeroed in on the crack forming in her facade. "What is it with you people anyway?"

Her eyes shot back to him. "What do you mean *'you people'*?"

"You people who live in this rarefied Vegas air," he said with a wave of his hand, indicating the extravagance of the empty restaurant. "You people have none of the touchstones normal, everyday folk do. You live in your daddy's casino castle, Jenna, playing with your glittery toys, fancy parties, little dogs. You're immune to the world. To reality. I don't think Candace's death means a whole lot to you."

Jenna's cheeks went red, his comments cutting to the quick and infuriating her. Lex clearly didn't like a single thing about her or her family. And quite honestly, when her father had asked her to come up with the auction shenanigan, Jenna hadn't thought of the ripple effects—the very real and dark implications down the road. Like having Lex's case thrown out of court and a killer walking free because of her. Or him losing his job.

Jenna couldn't help wondering what her dad *had* been thinking when he persuaded her to mess with Lex Duncan. Harold was renowned for his sharklike business acumen—he used people. God, was her own father using her, too? And why wouldn't he come clean about the provenance of that damn ring?

Jenna was convinced he wasn't telling her everything he knew about the history of that stone.

She suddenly felt scared and small. And stupid.

Like she used to as a kid.

Lex was right—she didn't have normal touchstones. She'd never had them. She'd been born into a family that always led her to believe the same rules that applied to everyone else did not apply to them. They were the Rothchilds, special, above it all.

"Wow, you really do have a problem with my family." She reached for her glass, took a deep sip of champagne, trying to hide her hurt. She'd be damned if she was going to let him see how badly he'd rattled her.

Guilt pinged through Lex.

He was lashing out at Jenna, making it personal, mostly because he was irritated with himself for being so damn attracted to this woman. For being weak. For falling under her bewitching spell.

He moved uncomfortably in his chair and suddenly felt the hard shape of The Tears of the Quetzal in his pocket. His pulse quickened at the reminder he still had it. What the hell had possessed him to take it? He had to get it back into lockup ASAP. Never mind Jenna and her games—if he lost a piece of evidence, a rock worth millions, he'd tank his own career all by himself.

The ring began to burn a hole into his conscience—and into his pocket—and an insane thought suddenly struck him. What if the ring had made him pocket it?

That was absurd. He was losing it. His body temperature elevated as the urgency to get out of this place and return the darn thing wound him tighter.

"You read me wrong, Lex," Jenna said sweetly, feeling anything but. He'd taken a mean jab at her, below the belt and personal. And now in her mounting anger, Jenna was growing even more determined to win. Because now this went straight to the core of her self-image, her secret vulnerabilities. There was just no way she was going to accept she couldn't seduce this man. And she sure wasn't going to leave here empty-handed, either. She was going to get the information her daddy wanted.

"I want Candace's homicide solved as much as you do, Lex. But I wasn't thinking about the investigation at all when I arranged the auction. I was thinking solely about charity, and entertainment. It's what I do—entertain. It's my job, and I'm good at it. And you saw what kind of money I raised." She smiled flirtatiously. "So why can't you just accept that and put business aside and enjoy a meal with me on behalf of your orphans?"

His gaze held hers, and the air between them began to vibrate with hot, dark tension. Something tightened in Jenna's stomach. Apparently he wasn't immune to her after all. And she felt a hot rush of pleasure. It fueled her determination. Heat began to pulse low in her belly, a shimmering excitement, anticipation welling inside her as she met the intensity in his sparkling, moss-green eyes. Right now, in the candlelight, they gleamed with the same hints of color she knew existed in the facets of The Tears of the Quetzal, if you held the stone just right. A strange, overly powerful sensation, came over her. It was so bizarre, so potent, she felt dizzy. Goosebumps broke out over her arms, and her heart began racing.

"Jenna? Are you all right?"

"I…um, yeah. I…I'm fine." She laughed lightly, unconvincingly. "For a second, I just felt as though…" *Some kind of ghost had walked over my grave.* "It was nothing. I just felt a little…dizzy. That's all." She blew out air, placing a hand on her chest, gathering herself. "To tell you the truth, I was thinking about The Tears of the Quetzal."

His brow lowered instantly, and his eyes sharpened forcefully. "What about it?"

"I—I was wondering where you're keeping it? Where is it now?"

He leaned back, studying her, the pulse at his jawline throbbing. He looked suddenly edgy. Dark and dangerous. "I thought you said no business. No more games."

She met his gaze, unflinching. God, he really was gorgeous. Suddenly she couldn't get the idea of sleeping with him out of her head. All she could think about was wrapping her legs around him, feeling his body against hers…inside hers. It was like she was possessed by a force beyond her control. "You know what I think, Lex," she whispered, her voice going husky as she leaned forward, showing him her cleavage, watching his eyes flicker downward with a small hot flare of female satisfaction. "I think you really do like to play games. You're a consummate poker player, aren't you, Lex?"

He forced his eyes away from her low-cut blouse, cleared his throat. "What makes you say that?"

"Because you're a watcher. I think you like to study people from the shadows, the sidelines, assessing weaknesses, while showing nothing of yourself. Then you suddenly take them by surprise." She sipped from her champagne glass, and his eyes dipped down to her lips. Jenna moved her fingers lightly down the stem of the glass, slanting her eyes back to his. "I suspect you know exactly how much a man can lose by carrying emotion in his eyes."

"You get this on *Dr. Phil?* I'm a cop, Jenna. Not a poker player."

"Same psychological posturing, same strategy, right? Whether it's casino chips or criminals."

He said nothing. Because she was right. Lex chose not to wear his heart on his sleeve, a skill honed from a very young age, right from that day in the closet. The day he saw his mother's throat being slit. The first day of his life alone.

Lex had come to realize that no matter what a man did in life, no matter what friends he made, no matter what women he slept with—or married—he'd always be alone. People were born alone and they died alone. Pain was suffered alone. Sure, he'd tried to convince himself otherwise. He'd gone and gotten himself hitched to a beautiful woman who'd said she loved him, tried the whole classic nuclear family thing. Been there. Done that. Didn't work.

It was a farce.

Now he just tried to be there for his at-risk kids whenever he could. But inside, Lex knew that, like him, they'd always be orphans. They'd always march alone. All he was doing was keeping them marching somewhere near the right track. Just like the old sheriff from Washoe County who'd stepped in to put him back on track when he'd started to run afoul of the law. That man had shown Lex he could take back control of his life.

Sheriff Tom McCall was *the* reason Lex had gone into law enforcement, a career Jenna Rothchild could end up costing him if he wasn't careful tonight. These thoughts suddenly chilled the edge off the lust simmering inside him. Sleeping with Jenna was not worth losing his life over. Because, in truth, that's what his job was—his life. It's all he really had, along with his charity work. Even his friends were all tied to law enforcement one way or another.

The food arrived, and a sommelier brought wine. They sat in awkward silence until the servers left again.

Lex took a deep slug of what was obviously a very fine merlot, but he was more interested in the numbing effect and getting this dinner over with than the vintage. It had taken strange turns and felt oddly personal.

Personal was not a place he cared to go.

"You still haven't told me what brought you back to Nevada, Lex," Jenna said between mouthfuls.

He stopped chewing. "Back?"

"I know you grew up in Reno."

"Rita told Cassie this?"

She nodded.

I swear I'm going to kill Perez.

Jenna dabbed her mouth with her napkin. "Cassie can be rather persuasive."

He grunted, chewing. The food was excellent, and Lex realized he was famished. "I was born in Reno," he said, slicing into his fillet. "My mother was a Vegas native."

"She's deceased, then?"

He held her eyes for a moment. "Yeah." He cleared his throat. "But I guess you know all that, too." He took another swig of merlot.

"I don't," she said, her big brown eyes softening with a genuine compassion. It made her more beautiful, and Lex had to tamp down a strange impulse to tell her this, to let her know that when she dropped the act, he actually saw something he really liked, beyond her body. "She died when I was five," he said, a weird compulsion driving him to tell Jenna things he'd really had no intention of revealing. "She was working at the Sun Sands Casino in Reno at the time, as a croupier. Before that, she worked here in Vegas, at Epstein's old place."

"As in *Mercedes* Epstein?"

"One and the same. Frank Epstein used to own the old Frontline Casino before he razed it to make way for the Desert Lion."

Jenna frowned. "It was Mercedes who forced your price sky-high at the auction, you know."

"And why do you think she did that, Jenna?"

"Probably to rattle the chains of the Rothchild clan—there's an old rivalry between Frank Epstein and my dad. She likely wanted to force me to fork over top dollar for her precious orphan charity. I mean—" she flushed. "I'm sorry, Lex, I know the charity is special to you. It is to Mercedes as well. She's known for her largesse when it comes to the Nevada Orphans Fund."

"So the Epstein-Rothchild feud runs deep. Why?"

She looked a little flustered. "I…I don't know. Honestly. My dad used to do business with Epstein back in the seventies. They had some kind of partnership deal. Then when my father wanted to move toward the construction of a couple of family-friendly super casinos, they had a falling out and parted ways. They won't speak to each other now. Not even in public." She brushed it aside with a quick wave of her hand. "But that's Vegas," she said, as if it explained everything.

Lex digested this information, wondering if the rivalry between the two casino moguls should be factored into his investigation. The FBI was looking for a motive—any motive—in Candace's death. It was the one thing the LVMPD, and now the FBI, could not get a handle on. At first they'd thought she was killed because of The Tears of the Quetzal, but then the ring had mysteriously shown up again in the purse of a single mother. Nothing about this case was making sense.

But Jenna artfully swung the focus back to him. "What happened to you, Lex, after your mother died? Did you stay with your dad?"

He snorted, a little light-headed from all the alcohol. "I have no idea who my father is. He might be alive, somewhere here in Vegas. He might be anywhere in the world or deceased himself."

Jenna studied him in silence for several beats. "I know what it's like," she said softly. "I mean, to lose a parent. I never knew my mother, either," she said. "She died giving birth to me."

"That must be some cross to bear."

She laughed, making light of it, but a telltale glimmer in her eyes gave her away. Lex felt a soft blush of affection, which startled him.

"Candace never let me forget it, either," Jenna said. "She was the mean twin. Natalie was cool, but when we were kids, and Candace and I fought, Candace would accuse me of 'killing' our mom." She shrugged. "I'm close to my dad, though. It makes up for it. Except…sometimes I think I remind him too much of June, my mother. I look a lot like her."

This was good, thought Lex. He was finally getting what he'd come for tonight—a better sense of family mechanics, of connections, of possible motives.

"So you didn't get along with Candace—you fought often?"

"Ah, don't think you can go looking at me for a murder motive, Agent Duncan." Her lips curved. "No business, just dinner, remember?"

"Touché." He smiled, in spite of himself.

"But *your* personal life we *can* talk about." She placed her hand over his. Nerves and heat skittered though him. Little warning bells began to clang at the back of his brain, but he found himself ignoring them as he turned his hand face-up under hers and traced his thumb across her palm. "I suspect," he said in a dark whisper. "That you're still playing me, Ms. Rothchild. And I'm still wondering why."

Her eyelids dipped. She moistened her lips, swallowed. "Would you like to go somewhere for dessert, Agent Duncan?" she whispered.

His heart kicked, then jackhammered. "You're proposi-tioning me?"

She said nothing, just looked direct into his eyes.

Heat speared into his groin. Panic circled.

He had to extricate himself. Fast. Before he did something real stupid.

He pulled his hand away abruptly. "It's late. I think I've upheld my end of the bargain." He plunked his napkin on the table, intending to get up.

"Wait." She grabbed his arm, forcing him back into his chair. He stared at her fingers on his arm, anxiety torquing. If he looked back into her eyes he'd be toast, and he knew it.

"You can't just leave like that."

"Why not? Or did you think plunking down a quarter of a million would buy bonus extras, Jenna? Like sex?"

She stared at him in stunned silence for several beats. "Oh, that's…harsh," she whispered.

"Well, then tell me exactly what you're doing here? Because you've been playing me like some high-class trick roller."

She opened her mouth, at a loss for words. *"Trick roller?"* She cursed softly. "That is *so* low."

"Then what the hell *do* you want from me?"

Raw hurt, then anger flared in her eyes. "You are so damn presumptuous!" she snapped. "I don't need to pay for sex with…with an uptight hunk of frigid granite." She pushed her chair back and got to her feet, taking the upper hand. "And don't think I'm going to let you be the one to walk on *me,* Duncan."

Jenna leaned down over the table, making sure he could see all the way down her shirt to her belly button, and liquid fire burned between his legs at the sight of her tight rose-brown nipples, firm breasts, flat stomach. She brushed her mouth angrily over his, aggressively parting his lips, flicking her tongue, ever so slightly, between them. A battle salvo.

Lex's heart raced. Her lips were soft. She tasted of wine. Dangerous. His world began to spin wildly.

"That—" she said, standing up, eyes flashing with fury…

and dark-hot desire "—is for free. Just so you know what you're missing, Agent Duncan."

"High-maintenance may be pretty on the outside, Jenna," he whispered, voice hoarse, his sudden erection straining against his pants. All he wanted to do was take her right here, right now, on this table. "Been there, done that. And I'll tell you something, Ms. Rothchild. It's not worth it."

She swore softly at him again. But it didn't hide the raw hurt glimmering in her eyes.

Then she swiveled and stormed out.

Lex slumped back in his chair. Beaten, hot and throbbing like he'd never been in his life. Angry as all hell at what he'd allowed to come out of his mouth. He'd been lashing out at himself for even being tempted. She was right. What he said was way below the belt. He didn't mean it. He watched her disappear into the restaurant elevator, silk pants swishing in smooth flow around her ankles. Dark hair swinging across her back. Head held proud.

The elevator doors slid shut, and the gentleman in him kicked back in.

Who the hell did he think he was?

He got up, ran after her, jabbed repeatedly at the elevator button, cursing the car to rise faster.

Jenna was shaking, hurt, aroused. Her eyes filled with tears. Never had she been through such a maelstrom, or been so humiliated. She was like a frustrated firecracker ready to detonate by the time she stormed through and out the lobby into the steaming Vegas night.

No one—*no one*—hurt her pride and dignity like that! But what really burned was the fact he didn't want her. That he'd been able to rein himself in. The coldhearted jerk was actually immune to her tried-and-true seductive ploys. To her wealth, to her looks.

She'd always gotten everything this way.

What cut even deeper were his comments about her lifestyle, her family. About who she was inside.

It made her want to prove him wrong. It made her want him even more, damn it. And that made her scared. Because she was beginning to see that if she really wanted to win Agent Lexington Duncan, she was going to have to try something completely foreign. She was going to have to be herself. That old self she'd buried at school so very many years ago.

So long ago that Jenna didn't know if that person even existed anymore.

What if there was nothing under her facade?

What if *this* was who she'd truly become?

She slumped back into the limo seat as her driver pulled into the street. Wouldn't that be ironic, she thought, if the one man in her life that she might actually end up wanting—really wanting—would be the one she couldn't have.

Lex rushed out under the myriad of gold bulbs just as Jenna's limo pulled out of the valet area and into the palm-lined boulevard of the sweltering Las Vegas night. He stared at the red brake lights flaring, then fading down the road. He swore, kicked a tire.

The valet came at him instantly. "Sir? Please—"

He raised his hands, backing off. "Sorry, sorry, no worries. I'm outta here," he muttered as he made his way to the line of waiting cabs. But as he stole another glance at the vanishing white limo, a dark sedan, plates obscured, pulled out fast, tucked in behind it.

Lex stilled, a sixth sense whispering inside him. The limo turned left off the boulevard. The dark sedan followed.

He shook off the sensation. It was Jenna's affect on his body—and it was the ring in his pocket messing with his head, making him paranoid. He climbed into a taxi, almost telling the driver to take him straight to the Vegas FBI field office before his brain kicked back into gear. He should go home first, get his own vehicle, then return the legendary ring ASAP. He'd be a fool to make the cabbie an outside witness to the fact he'd even been to the FBI offices this time of night.

But as Lex sank back into the car seat, hand in his pocket, fingering Harold Rothchild's diamond, he realized he'd crossed the line. Big time.

What in heaven had he gone and gotten himself into?

The Avenger.

That was his tag tonight, how he was going to think of himself for this leg of his mission. He tucked in behind the white limo, slowing as it turned into the driveway of the Rothchild mansion. The security guard Harold Rothchild had hired since the murder of his daughter waved the limo in through the gates.

The Avenger cut his engine and lights, watched from darkness across the street.

He now knew the FBI agent heading up the Candace Roth-child homicide investigation was seeing the youngest Rothchild heiress. This could get interesting. It held real potential—in any number of ways. Hot deliciousness snaked through him, making him hard. Death, he'd discovered, excited him. Ever since he'd taken the life of that Candace slut.

Killing her had made him powerful. Invincible. Determined to systematically wipe out the rest of the Rothchild scum from the earth, to get his hands on The Tears of the Quetzal. He wanted that ring, *needed* it.

For his father.

And in doing this, his father's death would finally be avenged.

The fact that Agent Duncan had a personal interest in Jenna Rothchild made him feel even more righteous about it all. Duncan had become his key opposing force. His enemy, stoppage—ever since Duncan had thwarted him, conspiring with that lawyer Conner Rothchild to throw him a fake ring to save a cheap stripper.

He turned the ignition. Vegas was all a game. A gamble.

Somebody won.

Somebody lost.

This time the winner would be him.

And this week, Jenna Jayne Rothchild would be the one to die.

Chapter 4

It was almost midday, temperatures spiking at 105 degrees. Oscillating waves of heat shimmered up from the road as Lex pulled his SUV into the palm-lined driveway of the Rothchild mansion, braking at the security booth at the gates.

He wound down his window, showed his shield. "FBI, for Mr. Rothchild." The security guard pressed a button on a newly installed intercom system, announcing the federal agent's presence. So much for the element of surprise, thought Lex as the gates rolled open.

He drove up the sun-bleached driveway, the Rothchild mansion looming into view. The architecture was Spanish-influenced—Moorish arches, red tiles, stuccoed walls that echoed the sun-baked tones of the surrounding Mojave Desert. Palms flanking the entrance rustled softly in the hot breeze.

A wall of heat slammed Lex as he got out of his vehicle. He made his way up the steps to the massive front door, noting a small security camera tucked into the portico, another aimed around the side of the house. All new since his last visit. Harold Rothchild was clearly feeling a tad nervous these days, perhaps taking the threat that had been made to the powerful Rothchild clan after Candace's murder a little more seriously but not so seriously that he'd hired bodyguards. Lex rang the doorbell.

His goal today was to interview Harold without encountering Jenna. Harry Quinn be damned.

According to Jenna, Harold had old business connections with Frank Epstein. Epstein, in turn, had Vegas mob associations that went back to the early seventies, and he was currently the subject of an SEC and FBI commercial crimes probe into an apparent New York Stock Exchange junk bond scam. If there were connections between the Epsteins and Rothchilds it could go to the heart of motive for murder. At this point, Lex wasn't ruling anything out.

He also wanted to press Harold again about the provenance of The Tears of the Quetzal. Lex was convinced the man was not coming clean on the history of the diamond for some reason.

Hot wind gusted, crackling through the ragged palm fronds as the big door to the mansion swung open wide. And there stood the one person he was seeking to avoid, wearing nothing but a scrap of bikini the colors of a Tequila Sunset, and just as damn intoxicating as a shot of the liquor to his system. The sight of her clean took his breath away.

"Jenna. I was…expecting your butler."

Jenna's lips curved, but no light reached into her eyes. "I didn't think I'd see you again so soon, Lex."

His eyes skimmed hungrily over her—couldn't help it. She was wearing crazy high heels that put a killer curve into her calves, seductive arches into her feet and a powerful punch to his gut. In her navel, a small little emerald green jewel winked. It took an embarrassing moment before he could wrench his attention away from it. He cursed softly to himself as the latent tension from last night's date quickly began to shimmer between them again.

"I presume you're here to apologize?" she asked.

He cleared his throat. "Actually, I'm here on business. I understand your father is in?"

Her mouth flattened slightly, some of the glimmer leaving her. "Fine." She stepped back, holding the door open but not far back enough so he didn't have to brush against her barely covered chest as he entered.

"Harold is out by the pool. Go through the hall and then through the wet bar over there," she said coolly, with a tilt of her chin.

It wasn't the first time Lex had been inside the Rothchild lair, but again, he couldn't help musing his entire house would pretty much fit inside just the hall alone. He started to make his way over the gleaming tiles but paused. "Look, Jenna," he said, swinging around. Mistake.

She was too close.

His brain headed completely south, and she could see it. A whisper of amusement toyed briefly with her mouth. Yet a hint of insecurity remained in her eyes. An insecurity that wasn't apparent last night.

He'd put it there.

Again, guilt twisted.

He cleared his throat again. "I am sorry about last night. I…I want to say thank you for all the trouble you went to, with the dinner, the restaurant, your very generous contribution to a charity I—"

"It was my pleasure, Lex." But no pleasure showed in her features. "I just wish…" Her voice faded slightly. "Sorry it was such torture for you."

Oh, boy, she didn't know the half of it. He ran his hand over his hair, feeling sweat prickle along his scalp, and was thankfully saved by the appearance of the Rothchild butler.

"Ah, Clive," Jenna said, clearly relieved herself. "Special Agent Lexington Duncan is here to see Harold. Can you please show him to the pool?"

Harold Rothchild had movie-star good looks, thought Lex as he shook the flamboyant casino mogul's hand and took a seat on the designer rattan furniture in the shade on the pool deck. It was cooler by the water, a sparkling oasis surrounded by palms, thick-leaved shrubs, carefully tended blooms of exotic color and scent. A sprinkler shot staccato arcs over the greenery.

"Nice out here," Lex said.

"I like working by the pool," Harold answered dryly, taking a seat himself. "So, a personal visit? Must be important. What can I do for you Special Agent Duncan?"

Lex cut to the point. "What can you tell me about the provenance of The Tears of the Quetzal?"

Harold sat back with a deep sigh. "We've been through this."

"I thought maybe your memory might have been jogged since the last time we spoke."

He studied Lex for a long moment. "It hasn't. I can't add anything to what I mentioned to the FBI before. The Tears of the Quetzal was handed down by my father, Joseph Rothchild. The stone apparently came from one of his South American operations."

"But you have no paperwork to show this?"

"Not a thing. All lost in a fire in his South American office, way back."

Jenna had been right about one thing last night: Lex was a consummate poker player. Reading people—every flicker of an eye, body movement, inflection of voice—was a skill he'd sharpened to almost sixth sense perfection as a homicide investigator. And that gut sense was telling him that while Harold might be a good liar he was not *that* good. And he was lying now. Lex made a mental note to check out the story around the alleged fire. There'd have to be a record somewhere.

Jenna appeared carrying a tray of iced teas, cubes of frozen water with mint clinking against sweating glass, distracting Lex instantly. He thanked the heavens she'd tossed a skimpy pool robe over her bikini, but it still hung open down the front.

He couldn't blame her for showing off her body. A figure like hers required effort, probably honed to perfection with daddy's health club membership. It wasn't a thing to be hidden.

But it sure didn't help his focus.

A hairy little dog scampered at her heels, and for the first time Lex laid eyes on the subject that had provided so much amusement and yipping back at the FBI office. Ugly thing, he thought, glancing down at it. The animal settled at Jenna's feet, the movement drawing Lex's attention down to her immaculately painted red toenails. They matched her fingernails, the ones that had trailed over his hand the night before. His pulse quickened at the memory, and he concentrated on the dog instead. The pedigreed mutt had a row of sharp little white teeth along the bottom of his jaw that jutted out over his top ones. And its black beady dog eyes were trained on him. A growl began at the back of the ugly animal's throat as Lex met its stare.

"Oh shush, Napoleon, it's just the police," Jenna chided, at the same time managing to put Lex in his place on the social ladder. "Iced tea, gentlemen?" she said with flourish and a dazzling smile. She'd recovered her composure—game clearly back on. Lex felt his adrenaline spike. Another hot gust crackled through dry palm fronds.

"Looks like he's mad," Lex said to the dog, trying to avoid staring as Jenna leaned forward to set a glass of tea in front of him.

"Oh, Napoleon? He can't help it. He always looks like that, even when we have company we *do* like." She set a glass beaded with perspiration in front of her father. "You shouldn't judge someone on their DNA, Lex. That's prejudice in my book. People can't help what they're born to look like. They don't pick the financial status of the families into which they're born, either."

She was digging at him for his comments about her family last night.

"It's a dog, not a person."

"Napoleon is a 'he.' Not an 'it.' Aren't you my little poochikins?" She bent down and scratched under that mean little chin, then looked up. "And Naps is as good as human to me. More affectionate and understanding than some people I've recently met." She was back to provocatively taunting him.

Lex glanced at Harold in growing desperation. "Is there somewhere we can…talk?"

"I keep no secrets from my daughter," Harold said, reaching for his glass of iced tea. "She might even have something to add." He sipped, watching Lex, shrewd blue eyes set in creased, tanned features as he calculated the situation. He was a dangerous man, thought Lex. And the only help Harold's daughter was going to be was in distracting him from the reason he'd come here.

Lex stole another glance at her. She was settling into a deck chair in the sun just near the table and well within his direct line of sight. The little jewel in her belly twinkled in the sunlight as she wiggled her fine butt into position and readjusted her bikini bottoms. Napoleon scuttled into the shade under her chair and glared at Lex.

She began to rub in sunscreen.

His blood pressure began to rise.

Harold smiled—the smug, knowing male smile of a powerful patriarch who knew exactly what a fine genetic specimen of daughter he had under his mansion roof. And what effect she was having on the FBI agent who had deigned to come question him.

That smile hardened something in Lex.

He was going to find something to nail this mogul, even if it went way back into the 1970s and had nothing to do with his daughter's murder, or that spooky ring. "You were saying…you have absolutely no paper trail to prove the origin of the ring."

"I have nothing I need to prove, Agent Duncan. I know where The Tears of the Quetzal came from, and that's good enough for me. I'm not looking to sell or have it appraised. Mostly I'd like it back in my safe. Where it belongs. It's caused enough trouble already."

"Can you tell me what year the fire was that destroyed The Tears of the Quetzal's paper trail?"

"Give my lawyer a call. He might have that on record somewhere."

Lex caught Jenna glance sharply at her dad and sensed a flare of tension between them. He filed this away.

"So all you do have in connection with the ring is some…mumbo jumbo about a curse?" Lex said, allowing a hint of derision into his voice.

"A Mayan legend that was passed down with the diamond. In the right hands, instant and true love follows. In the wrong hands—"

"Yeah, I heard, grave misfortune."

"You had any misfortune down at the field office yet, Agent Duncan?"

"If you're implying the ring is in the wrong hands, it's exactly where it needs to be, Mr. Rothchild, until this case is resolved."

A darkness flickered, very briefly, through Harold's eyes. Lex felt the tension wind tighter between Jenna and her father as Jenna stirred on the deck chair, eyes now fixed on her father.

The hot wind blew a little harder, ruffling fine strands of hair over her beautiful features. And Lex couldn't help but think of how the ring had actually felt hot in his pocket at dinner, and again the thought of sex with Jenna crawled through his mind.

If he didn't know better, he'd swear he'd been under the damn Mayan curse himself, unable to resist the power of her charms in the ring's presence. He was relieved to have been able to return it to lockup without further incident. Damn stupid move that was.

He glanced at his watch, changing tactics. "We asked you a while back if there was anyone you could think of who might have a motive to harm your daughter, Mr. Rothchild. You gave us a long list of Candace's boyfriends, exes, married men and the spouses who might have felt cheated by your daughter's various high-profile love affairs. Has anyone else come to mind since?"

"No," he said, too quickly. "No one. Apart from that Thomas Smythe."

"I see you've installed quite a bit of additional home security recently."

"The security measures are past due. Should have done it ages ago."

"So you haven't received any more notes threatening the Rothchilds?"

Again, that darkness seemed to shadow Harold's eyes, and his body stiffened slightly. "What're you implying? That I'd hide threats from the police? I wouldn't jeopardize my family that way."

"Just doing my job."

"If you were doing your job, Agent Duncan, you'd have found the man who sent the first note. And you'd have located Smythe and questioned him."

First note. It did imply more than one. Again, Lex filed the information, and again, he ignored the jab over Smythe.

"We have no indication at this point it was even a male who wrote the note," said Lex, removing his notebook. He flipped it open, jotted down a few notes of his own. He'd get Perez to dig up whatever she could on Harold's Las Vegas business history from the 1970s onward, looking for ties to Epstein and his mob cartel in particular. He'd also get Perez to check into Harold's allegations of a fire at his father's old South American mining headquarters. "You ever had a business partnership with Frank Epstein, Mr. Rothchild?" he asked as he jotted in his book.

Harold said nothing.

Lex looked up, waited.

"What does my personal business have to do with my daughter's murder or the ring theft?" His voice remained civil but slightly quieter. A small vein had risen along his temple. Lex had angered the notoriously quick-tempered mogul.

"Just covering the bases. I understand you've had some history with the old Epstein cartel."

Silence.

"And that you and Epstein parted on bad terms?"

Harold stood abruptly. "My business is not on the table for discussion. This interview is over."

"Doesn't matter what's on the table, Mr. Rothchild. If there is a vendetta against your family for some reason, bad business blood may be behind it. It could spell motive for murder. Revenge." Lex paused for effect, cool as trademark granite on the outside. "Wouldn't be the first time in Las Vegas history, now would it? We all know what kind of secrets were once buried out in that desert. Secrets that people might even to this day kill to keep buried. Epstein had…rather interesting connections."

Harold's voice was now dangerously quiet, the controlled expression on his face belied by the small bulging vein, the cords of tension at his neck. "If you're alluding to a Mafia past, I—"

Jenna sat up suddenly, swiveling her tanned legs over the side of the deck chair. "It *was* strange that Mercedes Epstein crashed my auction and bid against me like that, Dad."

Harold Rothchild cast his daughter a withering look.

Jenna met her father's eyes, a little pulse at her neck beating in pace with her heart, a small droplet of perspiration at the hollow of her throat glimmering in the sunlight.

Now, *this* was interesting.

Lex watched, still seated, while Harold stood glowering down at his daughter, but neither Jenna nor her father moved. It was then that Lex noticed the shadowy form of Harold's young trophy wife, Rebecca Lynn Rothchild, standing with a drink in her hand just inside the door of the wet bar, out of Harold's line of sight. Listening.

Rebecca Lynn caught Lex looking and moved quickly back into the cool shadows of the house.

Even more interesting.

Unfortunately this little domestic interplay was going to force Lex into further contact with Jenna. She looked to be a possible weak link in the family facade right now. A chink into which he was going to need to force his crowbar and leverage open. Just as Quinn wanted him to.

Lex already knew there'd been no love lost between Rebecca Lynn and Candace, who'd been close in age to Harold's newest wife. The LVMPD had looked closely at Rebecca Lynn as a possible person of interest in Candace's homicide because of it, but had uncovered nothing but a latent hostility. Lex wondered how well Jenna got on with her daddy's latest Mrs. Rothchild.

And by the look in Jenna eyes, not all was peaches between her and her daddy, right now, either.

Lex got to his feet, pocketing his notebook. "Thank you for your time, Jenna, Mr. Rothchild. I'll show myself out."

Harold moved in front of him, swift as a predatory mountain lion in spite of his age. He motioned with his hand, and Clive appeared as if from nowhere. "Actually, Agent Duncan, Clive will show you the door." He dismissed Lex with a curt nod of his silver head.

But as Lex entered the house, Harold called out behind him. "And you can forget pug-nosed mafiosos, Agent Duncan. Las Vegas cleaned up its mob act a long time ago, in case you hadn't noticed. The new Vegas has risen."

Yeah, right on top of dirty old mob money, thought Lex as Clive shut the massive front door behind him. The ghosts and secrets were buried in the same foundations.

Same snakes, different skin.

He was going to get Perez right onto checking with the FBI's economic crimes division in New York to see what they were digging up on Epstein. Might find more than one skeleton. More than one closet.

And he was beginning to think one of them might just belong to Harold Rothchild.

"You *do* know where The Tears of the Quetzal came from." Jenna glared at her father. "I swear I can tell by the way you answered Agent Duncan."

"I told you, Jenna, I can't say where it comes from."

"Can't, or *won't?* What's the deal with that rock, Dad? What're you trying to hide from me? And why?"

He checked his watch. "Are you going to be home for dinner, sweetheart? We can chat then. I've got a conference call coming in at—"

"Don't brush me off. Not this time. You were the one who asked me to get involved in this."

"Jenna, sweetheart—"

"That's always it, isn't it—Jenna, *sweetheart*. Your sweet

little Jenna Jayne, your youngest daughter who hero-worships her daddy and will do anything for him. Including seduce the cop on his case. Yet you won't treat me like an equal, like a damn adult, like you treat and talk to every other member of this godforsaken family!"

"Jenna!"

She stalked off on her heels, Napoleon scuttling after her.

"Jenna! Get back here! Where in hell is all this coming from all of a sudden?" He muttered a curse as she slammed the patio door shut behind her.

Jenna cinched her pool robe tightly across her waist as she stalked across the hall tiles and swung open the front door. She ran over the shimmering-hot driveway, reaching Lex's black SUV just as he was about to pull off. Banging on his driver's side window, she made a motion for him to open the window. A blast of cool air-conditioned air hit her face as he did. Jenna leaned forward into his window, the respite from heat welcome.

She'd set out to tempt and fluster him at the pool in retaliation for last night. And it had been working. But after listening to her dad, Jenna was feeling oddly vulnerable. Lex was right. While her auction stunt had started out as a stupid lark in her mind, it was no longer a game. And her dad wasn't being totally honest with her. Jenna was worried that even she was starting to look like a suspect to Lex. And if Lex ever found out that she had been at Candace's apartment—

Lex regarded her warily through the window, his green eyes crackling with suppressed fire, and suddenly Jenna was thrown right back to thoughts of the ring, the mysterious tones of burning green trapped inside the stone, and she clean lost her train of thought.

"What is it, Jenna?"

God, for the life of her she couldn't recall what she was going to say. Her head started to pound crazily, some magic in his eyes possessing her. And all she could think of was making a connection with him, seeking some reassurance from him that she'd see him again. "I…I know you don't approve of me, or my family, Lex. But…will you give me a second chance?"

His brow cocked up, confusion marring his rugged features. "That's why you came out here?"

She inhaled. "Let's just say I'd like to start over."

"There's nothing to start over, Jenna." He paused. "Is there?"

She swallowed, feeling compelled along this course now like a speeding car just waiting to hit the wrong hairpin bend. "Look, last night was not your thing, and neither was I. You made that pretty clear. But what *is* your thing, Lex. What makes you tick?"

A ghost of a smile toyed with the corners of his mouth. "You really don't like to lose, do you, Ms. Rothchild?"

She smiled. "Not if I can help it."

He studied her for several beats. "I tell you what. I'll show you my thing."

She flushed.

His hint of a smile cut suddenly into a wicked grin that made her heart do a slow tumble through her chest. It was the first time he'd actually smiled at her, and the effect was devastating. It totally blanked Jenna's mind of anything other than thoughts of being with him. Up close. Very close.

"I'll pick you up here tomorrow at noon."

"Where are we going?"

"That's when I'll show you what 'my thing' is." He put his vehicle in gear.

"But I'm working tomorrow."

He shrugged. "Too bad." He put his vehicle into drive. "It might've been fun."

"Wait!" She clasped her hands over the window edge of his door. "Okay…okay, I'll be here. Noon."

"Don't be late. I won't wait. Oh, and do me a favor, leave

little old Groucho Marx behind, will you." He shot a look at Napoleon. "I have a reputation to uphold."

Lex wheeled out of the estate gate wondering what he'd just let himself in for. He'd come up this driveway intent on keeping away from Jenna Jayne Rothchild. Now he was leaving, having made a date with her.

She's a tool. She handed herself to us on a silver platter with bonus cash to spare. You use that tool...

Yeah—but right now Lex felt that "tool" was somehow using him.

But in spite of that thought, as he neared the outskirts of town and drove down Lake Mead Boulevard toward the FBI building, he found himself grinning again.

Then he chuckled out loud at the thought of what he was going to show Jenna tomorrow. He was going to take princess out of her comfort zone, and he sure was going to enjoy seeing her as a fish out of water for a change. He'd purposefully not told her to dress real casual, either. That in itself was going to be entertaining—seeing her on his turf in those crazy whatever-inch heels.

A man needed every edge he could get.

Lex slowed his vehicle as he approached the guard hut at the FBI parking compound, realizing with mild surprise that Jenna's sense of fun, her sense of game, had actually infected him.

In spite of his caseload, in spite of everything else, he was feeling just a little lighter in his heart.

Jenna watched his SUV disappearing down the drive and ran her hands through her hair.

"Damn, what just happened here, Naps?" She stooped to pick up the one thing she trusted most in her world, and carried him inside. "Guess you better stay home and guard the fort for me tomorrow, because it looks like I have a real date with Agent Lex, and he doesn't want to share me."

She stopped suddenly, glanced up, thinking she'd caught a movement in one of the upstairs windows.

The drapes stirred. Then nothing.

Jenna frowned. *Must be the air-conditioning*, she thought. But as she started towards the stairs leading up to the front porch, Jenna caught a sudden glimpse of Rebecca Lynn ducking away from the window.

Jenna stilled and stared up at the window, a fusion of anger and disquiet rustling through her. *Daddy's obnoxious little trophy wife was spying on her again.*

Why?

The idea unsettled Jenna more than she cared to admit.

She climbed the stairs and let herself back inside. Despite her rush at being invited out by Lex, a cool sense of foreboding whispered through her.

Chapter 5

When they entered a rough neighborhood of housing projects, Jenna finally capitulated and asked, "Where are we going?"

"Right here," Lex said, turning into the parking lot of a school. He drove around the back of the building, came to a stop on a slab of cracked pavement under a lifeless tree, and killed the engine.

Jenna stared at Lex, then out the window.

A few banged-up old beaters were parked in the lot up against a chain-link fence in serious need of repair. Beyond the broken fence, on a field of drought-dry grass, a group of male teens, most of them built rough and tough, save for one real skinny guy, were running and tossing a football to each other under a scorching desert sun.

"The field is rutted, irrigation shot to hell," Lex said, opening his SUV door. "And a couple of the kids have to bus a fair way to get out here, but they do come. Twice a week." He came around to her door and opened it for her.

"Coming?"

A wave of sauna-like heat body-slammed into Jenna, clean sucking breath from her lungs, making her skin instantly damp. The white-hot glare of the midday sun was ferocious. She put on her massive designer shades. "You mean they come all the way out to this dead piece of field in this area of the city because of you?"

"Because of what *we* have built—a team. A sense of purpose. A friendship outside of their sometimes harsh lives. Those guys out there relate to each other, Jenna. They've all been through a similar thing—loss of family. Or they never really had one to begin with."

"So this is your volunteer job?"

"Not a job—" he began to walk towards a gate in the fence, his sports bag in hand "—I do it for love." He called back over his shoulder, "Coming?"

Jenna hesitated, loathe to leave the air-conditioned SUV. "So *this* is your 'thing'?" she called after him.

He stopped, turned to face her—rugged, tall, hair glinting in the hot sun. His rock-hard thighs were tanned, dusky, his calves powerful. In his shorts and workout gear, Jenna could see he was built just as rough and tough as any one of those young adult males out on the scorched field. He literally telegraphed physical prowess. Confidence. Leadership. And already his skin was sheened by a glow of perspiration. He looked even better than he had up on the stage that night. Bigger. Sexier. *Real.*

And way more at home.

"Yeah, Jenna. This is my thing. So? You gonna come meet the guys, watch us do some drills? Or d'you want to sit in the SUV?"

She stared at the dry field beyond the ugly fence, taking in the sandy patches among dead grass, the football posts. "It must be like 106 degrees out there, Lex," she said, pushing her thick fall of hair back from her face. "Why?"

"Why is it hot?"

"No, I mean, why do you coach at this time of year, this time of day? It's almost July. Midday. It's insane. People *die* exercising in weather like this."

A smirk played over his mouth as he raked his eyes slowly and purposefully over her short, tight skirt, her very high heels, the way her halter top was already wet with sweat under her breasts. "Can't stand the heat, sweetheart?"

Irritation flared. "Oh, please. I'm serious. People really do die in stuff like this."

"This is the only time we can get access to a field free of charge. No one uses these grounds at this time of day or on weekends. We take what we can get."

She thought of her quarter million donation. Of how it could help. Of why Lex had actually subjected himself to strutting on stage. While it had been a mercenary ploy on her part to help her father get his hands back on his precious ring, Lex had done it for those guys out there under the scorching sun on a burned-out field. His orphans.

He'd done it for love.

And she felt a little spurt of affection and of purpose. She—Jenna Rothchild—could actually help make a difference. A *real* difference.

To these lives.

To his.

She slammed the SUV door closed behind her, started toward him, careful not to catch her heels on the cracked concrete. "I still can't believe anyone actually physically exerts themselves in this heat," she muttered.

Lex grinned, and took her hand. As he did, a sharp jolt of energy whipped up her arm and slammed into her chest. Shocked, Jenna stopped dead, stared at him. And she could see in his unshaded eyes that he'd felt it, too. Again, thoughts of The

Tears of the Quetzal shimmered eerily into her mind as she stared into his green eyes. She felt shaken. And oh so out of place.

He glanced away sharply, equally rattled, and he started to lead her around the fence, making for a stand of metal risers along the perimeter of the field. Jenna stumbled after him, her sharp heels sinking deeply, awkwardly into bone-dry sand.

Jenna loved heels. They made her feel feminine. They made her feel complete when she dressed. But for the first time in her life, be damned, Lex was making her feel wrong in her own clothes. In her own city.

"You could have at least told me what to wear," she grumbled.

That smirk played over his mouth again, but he said nothing.

She stopped again, withdrawing her hand from his. "Oh, wait, I get it." She scooted her oversized designer shades higher up her nose. "You did this on purpose, didn't you?"

"What? You mean taking daddy's little casino princess out of her shiny tower and putting her down in the dirt? Showing her how real folk live on the other end of town? Now why would I want to do that?"

She glared at him.

His eyes sparkled, naked against the harsh glare.

The sound of a boot resounding off pigskin echoed over the field as one of the guys kicked the football, his skin gleaming ebony with sweat under the relentless sun. Another teen caught it, absorbing impact with his body, then ran. The others were doing exercise drills. But they all stopped, began milling about, watching from the distance as Lex and Jenna approached the risers.

She knew they had to be wondering who she was, why she was here. And for the first time since elementary school, before the girls decided she was "cool," Jenna actually felt self-conscious.

"Hey, Coach!" The guy with the ball yelled, punching his arm high into the sky.

Lex raised his hand. "Be right there!" He stopped at the risers. "You want to watch from here?"

She shielded her eyes. There was nowhere else, no shade in sight. "A hat, Lex. You could have suggested I bring a hat. And sunscreen."

He held out his duffel bag. "All in here. Ball cap, sunscreen, sports drink, water. Camera. The guys would love some shots of practice, if you're up to it."

Jenna wasn't sure whether to curse at him, call her father's chauffeur to come fetch her, or just show Lex that she could suck it up and take whatever curveball he was going to throw at her next. She grabbed the bag handles. "So, now I know what turns you on, Agent Duncan—making fun of *me*."

His gaze skimmed brazenly over her body. "It's just *one* of the things—" he said, lowering his voice "—that turns me on, Jenna."

Her nipples hardened in spite of the heat, and she swallowed. "Guess I asked for it, huh?" she said softly.

A delicious smile curved over his lips. "I guess you did, princess." He hooked his knuckle gently under her chin. "Would you prefer I take you home?"

"If I said yes, would you?"

He laughed—a glorious sound deep and throaty, from somewhere in his broad chest. It rippled over her skin, unsettling her further.

"What is so damn hilarious? Why are you laughing?"

"Because, Jenna." He tilted her chin up gently. "I *know* you won't say yes."

"A gambling man are you then?"

"Just an astute reader of personality. I think you pointed that out yourself over dinner. And you, Jenna, are a fighter. In your own sweet way."

"And you, Lex, are annoyingly patronizing," she snapped, as she yanked the bag from his hand and turned to climb the bleachers before realizing that in her tight skirt, she was going nowhere up. She was going to be relegated to the bottom rung. The universe was trying to tell her something today.

"Glad you find me so amusing," she said, dumping his bag down on the bottom riser. She rummaged through it, finding his water bottle, and she took a deep and thirsty swallow, wiping a spill from her mouth with the back of her wrist. "Still can't believe anyone can handle physical exertion in this hellish weather. I'll be the one sitting here saying I-told-you-so when one of your guys collapses and dies."

Lex pulled off his shirt, abs rippling, and Jenna stared while he wasn't looking. "My boys are built to take the knocks in life," he said, pulling on a fresh gray T-shirt that molded to his hard lines. "They wouldn't be here today if they weren't. Some of those guys have had a really rough shake, Jenna. They're lucky to even be alive."

"And they're all orphans?" She offered the water bottle to him.

He took a swig. "Yeah. Some are in foster homes now, being bounced around by the system. Others are on their own."

"Is that what happened to you, after your mother died? Were you bounced around the system?"

"Yup." He capped the bottle. "Until I ran afoul of the law in a minor way. I was on a one-way track to trouble until Tom McCall, the Washoe County sheriff at the time, took me aside and helped me pull my act together. He said he saw something in me." Lex hesitated for a moment, the darkness of some memory entering his eyes. "I ended up going into law enforcement because of Tom. He showed me that if I worked with the system, instead of against it, I could take charge. Hit back. Fix things."

"And catch bad guys."

He looked at her, silent for a beat, darkness consuming his eyes. "Yeah. And catch bad guys."

Jenna studied him, sensing a hidden story between his

words. She wondered which bad guy in particular might have fired up the young Lex and what it was he'd so badly needed to fix back then.

Lex turned to look at his boys out on the field. "I owe that sheriff," he said quietly, watching them for a moment. "Big time."

"And helping those kids is your way of paying back?"

He grunted, tossing the water bottle back into his bag. "We'll be out there for a couple hours. If you start to wilt, go wait in the car." He began to jog out onto the grass.

She swore at him, only partly in jest. He turned, jogging backward, a big grin back on his face. "Hey, Rothchild—I *like* fighters," he said. And he turned, jogged out onto the hot field to join his guys.

Jenna forced out a lungful of air as she plunked herself down on the metal bench. Yelping, she jumped right back up as the hot metal seared the backs of her legs under her short skirt. She cursed again, yanked Lex's shirt out of his bag and sat on it, thinking it was a darn good thing she'd listened to him and left Napoleon at home. Poor Naps would have perished of heatstroke out here. She might just die herself, she thought, wiping sweat from her brow with the back of her wrist.

As the minutes ticked by the day pressed more heavily down on Jenna. Her face grew flushed and red, her hair springy. Sweat trickled irritatingly between her breasts, down her stomach. But she was not going to let Lex win—she was *not* going to crawl back into his air-conditioned SUV with her tail between her legs. She refused to give him that satisfaction. She lifted the hem of her halter away from her belly and fluttered her shirt, trying to let air in and dry herself.

Nothing worked.

Jenna finally just gave in to the sweltering temperature, stopped worrying about what the humidity was doing to her hair, and how beet-red her face must be—no one cared what she looked like out here, anyway. So she let the heat swallow her as she watched the guys play.

Lex repeatedly threw the ball, neat spiraling rockets as the guys peeled off a line, one by one, to run and catch it. While they sweated they traded cheerful insults, bantering. Guy stuff. The day grew hotter, more intense.

Jenna shaded her eyes and squinted toward the distant mountains. The red haze over them was gathering into a dark bank of purple cloud, signs of a looming summer electrical storm. No wonder the air pressure felt so heavy.

Lex ran backward, received the ball and was tackled hard. She heard him thud to the ground.

Jenna winced.

But he was up, running and throwing again, his muscles getting pumped, his hair damp. His skin glistened, and his T-shirt molded wet to his torso. They played hard like that for almost a full hour, zigzagging over the field, doing different drills. Lex looked so different out there compared to the dry FBI suit who'd visited their home yesterday. On that field he was in his element, gripped by a sense of free spirit, joy even. It was fascinating to watch.

Jenna got over herself and into the spirit. She found Lex's camera in his bag, fiddled with it until she figured out how to use it. Then she kicked off her sandals and worked the sidelines barefoot, the grass hard and sharp underfoot in some places and pocked with small stones in others. But it was easier than having her spiked heels sinking erratically into soil—she was so not going to break her ankle. She could just imagine the hilarity that would invoke. He was asking for her to make a fool of herself, and she knew it.

Well, she was going to prove him wrong.

Jenna got down on her knee, her skirt riding high up her thigh. She zoomed in with the lens, clicked. Good shot, she thought, trying for a different angle.

Lex waved, suddenly distracted by her and what she was doing. It cost him—he took the full brunt of a barreling kid in the gut, blew backward into the dirt, landing with a hard bounce that made her scrunch up her face.

Ouch.

But he laughed—that great big infectious laugh. And she caught the moment on camera. Then she lowered her lens, stilled. He watched her for a moment, an energy transferring between them over the length of the field, crackling with soft electrical potential.

"Coach! Heads up! Incoming!"

He spun, caught the football just in time and the game was back on.

Jenna smiled.

Lex ducked his head under an outside tap, sun hot on his back as a barefooted Jenna watched. He stood, flicked back his wet hair. "Pass my shirt, will you?"

She handed him his clean T-shirt with a warm smile and a happy lightness in her eyes.

He stilled as he took his shirt. Something had shifted in Jenna. His princess had easily shed her Vegas glitz. She looked *real*—her hair a sexy wild mass, skin aglow, cheeks kissed soft pink from the sun, her blouse molded to her breasts, damp with perspiration—and Lex's world narrowed as his attention was drawn along the curves of her body. He slowly took his shirt from her hand, forgetting why he'd brought her out here in the first place. He forgot the homicide case, The Tears of the Quetzal, the FBI…it all flowed in a dim viscous river to some place deep down at the back of his mind as his skin connected with hers.

She came a little closer, eyelids lowering. "Lex—" her voice come out a low whisper "—I understand."

Lex tried to swallow. "Understand what?"

"What you don't like in me." Her eyes held his with a bright directness that made him turn to throbbing molten lead down low in his gut. The sun burned down on his head.

"I can see why I am not your thing," she said.

Right this minute, babe, you're exactly like my thing.

He cupped the side of her face suddenly, thumb under her jaw. And he tilted her full mouth up to him, meeting her lips with his, fast and hard before he could think. Her curvaceous body softened instantly against his. He drew her close to his naked chest, tasting her, drawing her scent in deep as he opened her soft, sweet mouth under his.

She ran her hand down his torso to his waist, urgency mounting in her body, and she reached the band of his shorts. A raw lust bottled and swelled inside him like it was going to blow. He wanted her bad. All of her. Now. Here. In his car, wherever. But this was wrong, so wrong…*the legal stuff will be in the clear as long as you keep your hands off her.*

He pulled back instantly, breathing hard, trying to align everything in his head—he was supposed to be working her for information, and he'd just crossed the line, damn it.

Quinn would have his balls if he found out. The system would eat him alive.

Lex swore to himself. No one needed to know this had happened between them. He just had to make damn sure it didn't happen again, and that he kept his lust in check. Besides, how could he be sure that Jenna wasn't still playing him on behalf of her father? He wouldn't put anything past that family.

Lex quickly pulled his shirt over his head, cleared his throat. "We should get into the shade. It's…hot."

"It sure is." She grinned. Genuine. Affectionate. Definitely not calculated. And deep down Lex wanted to believe that what he saw in her face, in her eyes, was real. And that's when he knew he was in real trouble. "Do…uh…you want to go get an ice cream…or something?" *Like a cold shower.*

"Love to."

"Hey, Coach!" The skinny kid suddenly came trotting back around the corner, all toothy smile and sweaty gear. "I lost my bus money."

"Again?"

"Could you maybe loan me some?"

Lex peeled off a couple of notes from his wallet and handed them to the kid. "You gotta watch your cash, Slim."

He shuffled on his feet. "Hey, I'll pay you back, just like I did last time."

"Yeah. Take it. Go." Lex slapped him playfully on the back. "Get yourself some dinner while you're at it. Put some meat on those skinny bones of yours."

"Thanks, Coach! Thanks a ton."

"Go!"

He spun and jogged off.

And in that moment, Jenna thought she could fall head over heels in love with this man. He was the furthest thing from any of the guys she'd ever dated, and way out of her social circle, but he did something to her. He'd make a terrific father, and that made her think that maybe she wanted a family of her own someday. Something real, built on love. And the notion shocked her. Jenna had never, ever thought along these lines before.

"Come," he said, taking her hand in his and leading her back to his car. "You surprised me back there, you know?"

"Because you thought I'd melt?"

"You did," he chuckled, holding the car door open for her.

Jenna flushed. He was right—she had melted. Her hair had frizzed out all over the place. She'd gotten sunburned and sweaty.

And she didn't give a damn. Because *he* thought she looked gorgeous. She could see it in his eyes. She'd tasted it in his kiss.

And that's all that mattered right now.

Afternoon was segueing into evening and wads of purplish-red clouds were now scudding in from across the Mojave as they entered an industrial part of the city. Jenna felt fatigue creeping up on her. With the low feeling came a sense of regret.

After watching Lex give of himself to those kids, after having seen him suffer on stage at her auction because he cared for them, Jenna was beginning to feel she was a flake. Truth be told, she'd wasted a good chunk of her life shopping and partying. Moving from one pseudoevent to the next. She was surprised Lex had even bothered to bring her out here, that he'd actually given her a second chance.

Why had he?

She glanced at his strong profile as he drove, and Jenna found herself wishing it was because he'd glimpsed something in her. More likely it was because he was interested in her connection to Candace—and his case—and he wanted to keep plying her for information.

He shot her a look. "Hey, what's up? You've gone quiet on me."

She shook her head, feeling a weird burn of emotion in her eyes. "It's nothing."

"Jenna?"

She looked out the window.

He drove in silence for a moment. "I'm sorry," he said. "For what happened back there."

"Oh, no, Lex…that's not it."

"You sure?" His eyes were vulnerable, and she felt a sharp stab of affection. It bloomed soft and warm through her chest. She tried to smile. "I was just thinking…about how I've wasted my life, my money. How I could've been doing so much more.

Seeing what you did in one afternoon, how you create a sense
of family for those kids…" Her voice faded as she thought of
her own dysfunctional family, that stupid woman her dad had
gone and married. About how she wished she'd had her real
mom around. "It's nothing."

"Hey, you haven't had a normal life, either, Jenna. Growing
up in Vegas, imprisoned by your father in that—"

Defensiveness flared in her. "Imprisoned? Hardly. And my
father has always been good to me."

"I know, I know. I'm sorry."

She shook her head, pulling a face. "It's okay. Lord knows
I probably deserve some payback considering the hell I put you
through at that auction."

Lex turned down a deserted street. The sky was lowering,
darkening over them, a strange kinetic energy filling in the air.
The torn fronds of a lone palm fluttered in the hot, mounting
wind. Litter scattered in squalls across the streets.

This section of town was a far cry from the glittering epi-
center of Jenna's existence. She began to feel nervous as they
passed lowbrow gambling halls, dim bars, a few homeless
people huddled in a corner, sharing a smoke. The streets seemed
strangely empty for a Saturday evening, compared to the 24/7
buzz that was the Strip.

Lex swerved to the curb suddenly and slammed on brakes,
his tires screeching.

"What is it?"

"I saw someone—" he rammed his SUV into reverse,
backed up a block, fast. Across the street an older woman in a
gypsy skirt walked briskly down the sidewalk, black shawl
fluttering in the wind. She turned and abruptly vanished into a
narrow alley.

"It's *her!*" He reversed farther.

"*Who?*"

He turned the ignition off. "Jenna, I need to check something out. Can you wait?"

Nerves fluttered irrationally in her stomach. She glanced out the window at the darkening street. The first fat plops of rain were beginning to fall. "What is it, Lex? Who was that woman?"

"Someone I've been looking to question for months. Every time I come out this way, I seem to miss her, like ships that pass in the night. I won't be long."

Jenna sat in the SUV as he jogged across the road and disappeared down the same alley that had swallowed the woman. Craning her neck to see over the backseat, Jenna tried to peer down the alley and caught the flutter of the woman's shawl as she vanished into a tiny storefront that had a broken pink neon sign over the door. Jenna could make out the first two words: Lucky Lady. The *c* was missing.

Hot wind gusted outside more fiercely. Bits of newspaper swirled off the sidewalk and danced up in a wicked little dervish. The sky turned a deeper purple. A man pushing a shopping cart wandered by, stared at her.

Jenna double-checked that the doors were locked.

But after a few minutes, she was feeling real uneasy. The streets were growing eerie with the dusky dark orange glow of the coming storm. Heavier drops of rain bulleted down onto the car.

Jenna reached for the door handle. There was no way she was going to sit here alone in a full-blown storm. Then she hesitated. Few places in the world had tighter security than the big resort hotels clustered in downtown Vegas. But outside those populated tourist areas Sin City had the same urban ills and muggings as any other big metropolis. Common sense had always had Jenna sticking to the busy parts of town, the well-lit streets.

These were not.

She removed her ostentatious emerald bracelet and the

diamond pendant around her neck, then opened Lex's glove compartment. But as she was about to stuff them in, she saw a plastic sleeve containing old newspaper cuttings. One headline immediately caught her eye: "Reno Mother Brutally Slain While Son Hid in Closet."

Curiosity quickened through her. Wind rocked the vehicle slightly, and Jenna grew edgy as she scanned the news cutting. But as the words of the report sunk in, her blood turned to ice.

It was a story printed in the *Reno Daily* thirty years ago about a croupier named Sara Duncan—a single mother aged twenty-seven who'd been slain in her own home while her five-year-old son, Lexington Duncan, had hidden in the bedroom closet.

Jenna quickly read the second article contained in the plastic sleeve. Sara's child had actually witnessed his mother's throat being slit through the louvered slats of the door, but had not been able to speak for well over a year. And when he had started speaking again, Reno police learned he was unable to identify his mother's killer. He'd only seen the man's pant legs and hands. And the knife—the murder weapon used to cut Sara Duncan's throat.

Jenna sat back in her seat, numb.

Lex wasn't just an orphan. His mother had been taken from him in the most brutal way possible.

And he'd *seen* it.

Suddenly she felt scared. Alone. And beyond curious. She opened the car door quickly. Rain was coming down hard now, the kind of torrential summer downpour that flash flooded Vegas streets notorious for bad drainage, snarling traffic up along the city arteries.

She ran across the street and ducked down the alley.

Chapter 6

Small bells chinked as Lex entered the Lucky Lady psychic store, tendrils of incense smoke curling in the wake of his movement. It was dim inside—no air-conditioning. Shelves cluttered with silver dragons, cards, dice, engraved boxes, fetishes, crystal balls and fat little Buddhas lined the walls.

This was obviously the Lucky Lady's game—peddling fortune, fate, magic. Selling a chance to beat the odds, win the dream. Parting cash from those who believed they could control such things. Lex's eyes adjusted to the light, his gaze settling on a faded old poster that hung on the far wall. It promoted a topless, psychic act at the old Frontline Casino circa 1970s, the same casino his mother worked at. The "psychic" on the poster was a busty, leggy redhead in a belly-dancer costume, shown seductively stripping copious veils.

"Hello!" Lex called out. "Is there anyone here?"

A parrot squawked somewhere in the back. Lex tensed. "Hello?"

Suddenly, from behind a heavy curtain sewn with a myriad of tiny silver stars, the old gypsy woman he'd seen on the street materialized. Lex's pulse quickened. She came slowly forward, huge false eyelashes making her unblinking eyes seem surreal. Gold hoop earrings dangled from her ears and small spots of rouge looked comical on her parched cheeks. Her wrinkled eyelids were heavily lacquered with blue-green eye shadow, the color collecting into darker rivers in the creases of her aging skin. Lex realized with a start that she was the woman depicted in the old poster, faded and crumpled and made sadly comical by time as she tried to hold on to the thinning threads of the past.

"Marion Robb?" he asked.

She blinked. "Who's asking?"

"I'm Lex Duncan," he said, wondering what this woman could possibly tell him. "A friend of mine, Tom McCall—the old Washoe County sheriff—said I might find you here. He… suggested I come talk to you."

Her features grew guarded. "What does the sheriff's office want?" Her voice was husky, the sound of possibly too many cigarettes, cheap whiskey and loud bars.

"McCall is retired. He doesn't want anything, it's me who—"

"You a cop?"

"I'm here for personal reasons."

"You are a cop then."

"FBI."

"What? You want a reading?" She jerked her head toward her rate board. "I'm about to close up shop, but I can maybe do a fifteen-minute session."

The parrot squawked again, and thunder rumbled low and close outside. Lex could hear the splat of rain coming down heavily out in the street. A gust of moisture-tinged air chased through the store, and a door somewhere banged upstairs.

Lex cleared his throat. "I didn't come for a reading, ma'am. Tom McCall told me that you once knew Sara Duncan, a croupier who worked at the old Frontline Casino about thirty years ago."

Her face remained expressionless, but he detected a shift in her body tension. "What you say your name was?"

"Lex Duncan."

She stared at him for a long while, and as Lex watched, her features seemed to melt, and her hand went to her neck. "My oath," she whispered, voice hoarse and low. "You're her boy."

Lex's chest constricted, his mouth going dry. "I…wanted to ask you some questions about Sara, about my mother. Sheriff McCall helped work my mother's homicide case along with the Reno police all those years ago. He mentioned you had been a friend of my mother's, that you and her used to work together at Frank Epstein's Frontline Casino."

She nodded. "Before it was razed to make way for the Desert Lion. Yes. Yes, I worked there at the same time Sara was there." She drew the curtain back hastily, hooking it up into a silver loop. She pulled out a chair at a small round table that was draped in midnight-blue velvet. "Sit." She fluttered her hand full of rings at the chair.

He held up his palms. "I didn't come for a reading—"

"No, no…you must sit."

Lex edged awkwardly onto the tiny chair at the little round séance table. The old woman seated herself opposite him, reached over the table, clasped both his hands in hers, her skin papery, dry, her fingers bony. "I can't believe it," she whispered. "Sara Duncan's boy." Moisture filled her eyes as she considered him intently. "You have her features, you know? And the color of your eyes, it's the same green as hers. Sara, she turned the head of many a man…you've come looking for your father."

Lex shook the chill she gave him. It would be obvious that he'd be looking. "Yes," he said.

Always, he was looking.

She narrowed her eyes. "But mostly you want the man who killed your mother."

He said nothing.

She sighed heavily. "Son, you're seeking a past in a city that holds no memory. Not only that but there are still people in this town who will go to great lengths to ensure that the past stays where it belongs—buried." She leaned forward, bony fingers tightening around his. "You go trying to mess with that, and you're looking to be messing with some real bad ghosts."

"I'm looking for truth. Not ghosts."

She shook her head. "Honey, what you're looking for is trouble."

Lex heard the storefront bells tinkle suddenly, as if someone had entered the store. He couldn't see the door from where he was sitting—he was tucked behind the curtain. Besides, he couldn't tear his eyes away from the woman's strange, lined face. Probably just another gust from the storm, he told himself. The bells blew again in the wind. Thunder clapped right overhead. Candles shimmered, sputtered in wax. His pulse quickened. "What are you trying to tell me?" he said quietly.

She closed her eyes, began to rock backward and forward, her voice taking on a strange and dissonant monotone. "A past…buried in the Mojave sands. Sands of time…a grave…"

"What *exactly* are you saying?"

She rocked some more. Then her eyes suddenly flared open. "Bodies!" she hissed.

Tension wedged into Lex's throat. "Look, I didn't want any reading. I just wanted to ask you some questions about my mother."

Her eyes refocused on him. "People used to bury bodies

out there, in the desert, you know? Before the feds ran them out of town."

People? Feds? Was she alluding to the fact he was a federal agent, or was she referring to Las Vegas's dark mob past? Lex thought of the fat envelope of cash that used to arrive for his mother, delivered by a guy in a shiny blue Cadillac convertible. "Are you trying to say my mother might have been involved with organized crime?"

"Everyone—" she whispered "—was touched by those tendrils of evil. Everyone."

Lex grew agitated. He didn't believe in this woo woo crap, yet this woman was managing to rattle his cage nevertheless. He tried to get back on track. "Did Frank Epstein ever mess with my mother, while she was working there?"

She shook her head. "Don't even go thinking about it. Epstein is not your father. He used to bed a different woman every night, but once he met his Mercedes, then a showgirl from the Flamingo Club, his whole world changed. From the moment he laid eyes on Mercedes he never, ever touched another dame. And he never touched your mother."

"Why did Sara leave Vegas after she was fired from the Frontline?"

"I honestly don't know. She just packed up one day and vanished." A sadness filtered into the Lucky Lady's eyes. "I figured it was because you were on the way. Maybe she wanted a fresh start."

"She wasn't seeing someone special in Vegas at the time?"

"Lexington, I loved your mother. We were close, real close. Like sisters. You need friends in a town like this, and she was mine. But not once did she talk about a special man in her life, and I never saw her with anyone who might be special to her."

Lex was startled by her use of his full name. No one but his mother had ever called him Lexington.

"Sara broke my heart, you know, when she left? Took me almost a year to learn she'd actually ended up in Reno. By then you were born. I visited her a couple times, but she was different…distant. She was getting regular money from some place. I reckon she must've had a decent gig going because she bought her own house in a Reno suburb, never talked about Vegas." She inhaled deeply. "Look, maybe she was seeing a married guy and he was paying her to keep quiet about his kid. Or maybe she was hooking again, high-class stuff." She met his eyes. "I would tell you if I knew who your father might be, Lexington. It was terrible what happened to her. Just terrible."

"You think my father might have killed her?"

"I don't know. And that's what I told the cops when they came to question me. They came because I was her friend."

Lex leaned forward. "Marion, my mother used to get cash, once a month, delivered by some guy in a pale metallic-blue Cadillac convertible. The car had a little sticker on the bumper, like a logo. It looked like cartoon lion standing up, with a crown on his head? Do you recall anyone who drove a car with a sticker like that? Maybe from the Frontline?" It wasn't something Lex had thought to tell the police when he was five. He hadn't even remembered that bumper sticker until very recently when he'd gone to see a woman the FBI occasionally used as a forensic hypnotist to aid witnesses in recalling crime detail. He'd done it because there was this hole in his life—this need to know what had happened that day, thirty years ago, and why. Because not once since that horrific moment had Lex stopped searching for the man with the sandpapery voice who'd slaughtered his beautiful young mother.

It had become a driving force in him.

It was why he was back in Vegas. And while he was here, he was going to keep looking. Until he found that man.

Dead or alive.

And this time, if that killer was still alive, Lex *would* be able to move. Instead of being frozen with fear in a cupboard. He now had a badge, and he had a gun. And he had the power to take the man's freedom. He was going to fix what he hadn't been able to fix three decades ago.

But the woman's face had suddenly shuttered at the mention of the Cadillac and bumper sticker. Her eyes grew flat. "That's all I know."

Lex sensed there was more. A lot more. He also sensed he wasn't going to get it by pushing. He'd come back again in a few days, win her confidence in increments. He had time on his side now. As long as he held this Vegas post.

He jutted his chin toward the faded old poster behind the woman, the one promoting the sexy topless psychic act at the Frontline Casino. "Is that you?"

"Back in the day."

"Nice."

She didn't smile.

Lex placed a wad of cash on the table. The woman stared at it.

"Please, Marion, take it. And thank you." He placed his hand on the wad, pushed it closer to her.

She closed her eyes suddenly and slapped her hand down hard over his, on top of the wad of notes, making him jolt. "A diamond!"

"What?"

"I see a diamond…a *big* diamond. Tears."

An ice-cold shiver rippled over Lex's skin. Damn, this woman really was psychic. "What about a diamond?" His voice came out slightly hoarse.

"Very, very powerful stone…" She began rocking again, faster, harder. "Great danger…. No! Great love. A curse and a promise wrapped in…*death…*" Her voice started to fade to a thin papery whisper. "Death…buried in sands…sands of time…death to be *avenged…*" Her eyes opened. She said nothing more. Just stared at him, features a blank slate. It was as if the woman inside the body was gone.

Hiding his uneasiness, he got up. "Uh…thank you."

"Be careful," she hissed.

"I…I don't believe in this stuff." He felt compelled to say it. To convince himself, more than her. Being involved with that Mayan rock of the Rothchilds' was getting to him.

"You can't *not* believe," she whispered. "You can't work in Vegas for any length of time without coming to believe, at some point, that luck, fortune, fetish, fate play a role in all of our lives. No matter how you try to control your destiny, Lexington, you can't not believe in magic. Not in Vegas."

Oh, yeah, he could not believe if he wanted to.

But his blood still ran cold as he stalked toward the store exit, needing to get the hell out of here, and fast. But he did a sharp double take when he saw Jenna standing wide-eyed near the door.

He grabbed her arm. "Geez, Jenna, how long have you been standing there listening?" he snapped.

"Did you hear what she said? About The Tears of the Quetzal?"

"Keep your voice down," he growled as he ushered her out into the pelting sheet of rain. They ducked their heads against the deluge, ran hand in hand to the car, got in breathless and wet. Both sat in silence for a moment.

Jenna turned to him. "Lex, she *had* to be talking about The Tears of the Quetzal."

"It was nonsense," he said brusquely. "And even if she was referring to the ring, it was probably because she read about Candace's murder and the diamond in the papers. Damn it—" he ran his hand over his rain-soaked hair "—she probably recognized me from the newspapers the minute I walked in there, played me all along. And then *you* go and walk in." Anger stirred, and he swore again. "If she goes to the press with this now, if she tells the media that you and I were together in that place, after they splashed me kissing you on that front cover—" Lex slapped the steering wheel.

"Lex—"

He turned the ignition. "You should have stayed in the damn SUV."

He pulled into the street, incensed. It was dark now, wipers smearing rain across the windshield. He'd be a fool to believe a word of what the Lucky Lady had said about his mother. The woman was a charlatan, a fake, like the rest of this place and everyone else in it.

Hands tight on the wheel, Lex replayed the scene in his mind, thinking of when exactly he'd heard the chink of bells and sensed another presence in the store. "You heard everything, didn't you? You heard me talk about my mother." His words came out bitter. He didn't want Jenna to know.

It was personal. Maybe a part of him felt humiliated by his past, the fact his mother had once been a hooker before she'd cleaned up her act and gone to dealers' school. Maybe a part of him really wanted all the ugliness of Sara's murder to stay buried, not associated with him. Hell knew. He'd never analyzed it.

"I already knew about your mother, Lex," Jenna said softly as she opened the glove compartment. "I saw these."

"Oh, you went snooping around my—"

"I didn't want to get mugged wearing my emerald bracelet and diamond pendant, okay? So I took them off to stash in here." She removed her bracelet from the glove compartment, clasping it back on while she spoke. "And I couldn't help seeing these newspaper cuttings."

"So you just read them."

"Wouldn't you?" she snapped.

He shot her a hard look. "Put them back."

She stared at him in silence for a moment, then shoved the

articles back into the glove compartment, slapped it closed. Lex noticed her hands were trembling.

They drove in tense silence, entering thickening traffic, water writhing little snakes over the windshield, refracting the brake lights ahead.

Then suddenly, in the dark, he felt her hand move onto his knee. Just a gentle touch. No pressure. Reassuring. Compassionate. As if to let him know she was there for him, that she understood.

Moisture burned suddenly into his eyes. His jaw tightened. He clenched his fists around the wheel. He needed to get her home, dump her outside her fancy mansion and get her the hell out of his life.

Because he was scared. He was starting to feel like leaning on her, sharing.

His deep down private stuff.

He didn't want another relationship, marriage. He didn't want to start falling for a woman—not in that way. *Especially* not Jenna Rothchild.

He remained silent as he drove sharply into her driveway. Waved on by the security guard, he drove right up to the portico, stopped, but did not kill the engine.

"I can let myself out."

He nodded.

She reached for the door handle, hesitated. "That's why you really came back to Vegas, isn't it, Lex?" she said. "That's why you put in for the transfer. You came to find your father. To learn who killed your mother." Her voice was thick, full of emotion and compassion. Lex just wanted to stay on safe, uncommitted territory. He wanted to cruise in his emotionally neutral zone. He wanted her to get out. Leave him alone.

"Yeah," he said, not looking at her. "That's why I put in for the transfer."

"Do you think that Mercedes Epstein bidding on you at the

auction had anything to do with…with the past, with your mother's job at the Frontline?"

"Why the hell should it?" Truth was, that question really unsettled him. "Mercedes showing up at your auction probably has more to do with the old business your father had with Frank Epstein, Jenna, than anything to do with me."

She stared at him in silence, opened the door. The interior light flared on and droplets of rain blew inside. But she wavered again.

"Lex?"

"What?"

"Thank you."

"For what?"

"For showing me something about myself that I'd forgotten today. It meant a lot to me, being with you. And those kids."

Lex didn't trust himself to speak right now, so he said nothing.

She leaned forward suddenly, kissed him fast and light on the mouth, and was gone, door slamming shut as she ducked through the rain and ran up the stairs. Clive swung open the door for her, and she was swallowed by her mansion as it closed.

Lex shut his eyes for a nanosecond, still tasting her on this mouth. He inhaled deep.

He was a cop.

He'd acted like an idiot.

Enough games.

He'd crossed too many lines, and now he had to pull back. But as he drove out of the Rothchild driveway in the pelting storm, he knew that he'd already gone too far.

Because deep, deep down, a part of him knew that he was falling for Jenna.

In spite of himself.

Jenna crouched down in the hallway to ruffle Napoleon's fur as he squiggled about her feet, happy to have her home. But as she petted her dog, she sensed a presence, someone watching from within the darkened interior of the adjacent living room.

She stilled, got slowly to her feet, walked into the dark room. "Hello?" she said, reaching for the switch of a lamp.

"Jenna." Rebecca Lynn's voice came from near the bar.

Jenna flicked on the lamp, saw her so-called stepmother sitting in a chair in front of the floor-to-ceiling window. From that window she'd have seen Lex's SUV, possibly even Jenna kissing the agent, illuminated by the vehicle's interior light because the door had been partially open at that point.

"Rebecca Lynn," Jenna said coolly. "Why are you sitting in the dark? Is Ricky in bed already?"

Ricky was Harold's newest child, his first with Rebecca Lynn, and his only son. Little Ricky was a spoiled kid, constantly being used as a bargaining chip in the relationship between Harold and his latest wife. A relationship that was going sour. Already.

"I was watching…the storm," Rebecca Lynn said.

Jenna realized from the studied delivery of Rebecca Lynn's words that her stepmother had already been drinking. Quite a bit.

"Was that the federal agent who dropped you off?" she asked. "The one on Candace's case?"

"Why do ask?" Jenna said, recalling the movement in the drapes upstairs after she'd dashed out to Lex's SUV yesterday.

She sighed dramatically. "Your father is hiding things from you, Jenna. Do you know that?"

Here we go again, trying to drive a wedge between me and my dad. "Look, I don't have time for this, Rebecca—"

"Oh, I think you do." She pushed herself up out of the chair, wobbled, smiled, then teetered over to the bar. She poured a heavy shot of gin, topped it with tonic and plopped a slice of lemon in, stirring it with her pinky. "I'd be surprised if that FBI agent doesn't think *you* could have done it."

"Done what?"

"Murdered Candace."

"Oh, for God's sake, are you insane? Or is that the gin talking again?"

"Hmm." She sucked the moisture off her pinky. "I did happen to tell the FBI there was no love lost between you and Candace, you know? I told them that when they questioned me the first time around. And then—" she took a sip from her glass "—Agent Duncan came to see me at work this morning. He asked me again about your relationship with Candace. Did he tell you *that,* Jenna?"

A cold chill seeped through her. Lex hadn't mentioned it.

"He didn't, did he?"

The feeling deepened. "Why should he? It's his case, he can't talk about the details with me."

"He's using you, Jenna Jayne, to get inside the Rothchild cloak of secrecy." She made a woo woo motion with her hands.

"Nonsense—I was the one who set him up at the auction remember?"

"At whose request, I wonder?"

"Well, that should prove a point, shouldn't it? The Rothchilds are the ones using him, not vice versa." Hell, why had she even said that? Rebecca Lynn was baiting her and fool that Jenna was, she'd taken the lure. Hook, line and sinker.

"I forgot to mention *that* fact to Agent Duncan this morning. Maybe," Rebecca Lynn said slowly, her words slurring, "I'll give him a call later and tell him that Harold requested you to go all out to seduce him for information on The Tears of the Quetzal."

Anger began to mushroom inside Jenna. "Do what the hell you like, Rebecca! You're drunk, and I'm going to change. I'm soaked." She turned to leave.

"I also know that you went to visit Candace on the night she was killed," she called out.

Jenna froze.

"Maybe, Jenna Jayne, if I was truly malicious, I might suggest the FBI try and match your DNA to the scene. Who knows what the feds could come up with."

Her heart jackhammering, Jenna turned slowly to face her wicked little stepmother. "You don't know what you're saying—"

"Jenna, I *know* you were there."

Jenna stared at Rebecca Lynn for several beats, feeling increasingly ill. Slowly, she sunk down into a chair, Napoleon at her feet. "How?" she whispered, scared now, wondering what Lex really knew about the night of the murder, wondering if this reviled stepmother of hers had already told Lex that she'd been at Candace's apartment mere hours before her sister was killed.

"*How* do you know?"

Rebecca Lynn started sashaying theatrically out of the room.

"Rebecca Lynn!"

She stopped in the doorway, smiling crookedly.

"Did you have me followed that night?"

"No, I went to visit Candace myself that night, Jenna. When I got there, I saw your car was already parked outside. So I just sat in my vehicle for a while, waiting for you to come out. Watching."

"What on earth were you doing there?"

"I needed to talk to Candace, alone. About…an issue between us. But then I saw you two up in front of the big lighted window, arguing. I saw Candace throw the vase at you, and you ducked. You began to pick up the broken pieces. It looked, Jenna, like you might have cut your finger, because you sucked it quickly. Do you think you might have left blood on one of those vase pieces? Your DNA, perhaps?"

Jenna swallowed against the thickness ballooning in her throat. She should have told the cops right away that she'd gone to try and talk Candace into a rehab program. But there was such a media circus around the murder she didn't want to smear her dead sister's name further into the mire. As much as she and Candace had squabbled, Candace was still her blood. Her *sister.* And there were her boys to think about. Jenna had been raised to close ranks at times of family trouble.

Besides, she knew she hadn't killed her sister, so what difference did it make, truly, that she'd been there a few hours earlier? Except now Lex would see it as a lie by omission. Another reason not to trust her.

God, he might even think she'd done it.

"Are you going to tell Agent Duncan?" she whispered.

"Don't think I need to. Your sexy bachelor agent probably already knows that you're a lying little bitch. It's probably why he's escorting you around town, plying you for information so he can nail you." She snorted derisively at Jenna's expression. "What? You thought he actually fancied you?"

Nausea slicked through Jenna's stomach.

If what Rebecca Lynn said was true—and Lex *had* been playing her—it meant the fragile bond she'd felt dawning between her and Lex today had been a complete farce. And that hurt more than anything.

Rebecca Lynn had just stomped her stiletto into Jenna's fragile burgeoning emotions, grinding them right into the dirt. And Jenna hated her more than ever. "You know I didn't hurt Candace," she said quietly. "If you were watching, you'd have seen me leave, while she was still alive. You're a witness to my innocence."

"Hmm," Rebecca Lynn said, putting the glass to her mouth, wetting her lips with gin. "Not sure I can recall those little details."

Jenna launched to her feet. "For all I know *you* did it! You've just told me you were there. *After* I was."

"I never went into her apartment. It would've been pointless to try and talk to Candace when she was in a drunken rage, so I drove home."

Jenna glowered at Rebecca Lynn, all sorts of dark suspicions suddenly growing in her mind.

Rebecca Lynn sighed theatrically, as if suddenly bored out of her skull. "I didn't hurt Candace, my dear, as much as I would've liked to," she said. "And I certainly didn't send all those threatening notes."

"There was only one note. A typed one, left in Dad's mailbox."

"Oh, really?" Rebecca Lynn glanced pointedly at Harold's study door. Jenna followed her gaze and noticed that the door was ajar. It was never open. Harold always kept that door shut. And through the open door Jenna could see the top drawer of his desk was partially open. Harold was meticulous about such things. He'd never have left it like that.

Had Rebecca Lynn been in there? Jenna shot a hard look at her inebriated stepmother. Rebecca grinned lopsidedly, held up her glass in cheers and sauntered out into the hallway, listing like a drunken sailor.

Whatever had possessed her father to marry that 34-year-old witch was beyond Jenna. She waited until she heard Rebecca Lynn's heels on the marble stairs, then Jenna went to her dad's office.

She clicked on the tiny desk light, worried that if her father returned, he'd see a brighter light from the bottom of the driveway.

She pulled the top drawer open wider. Wind lashed outside suddenly, drumming rain against the window in waves. The palm trees swished eerily against glass panes and the curtain billowed. Jenna tensed, her heart racing.

She was feeling spooked, guilty for being in here at all.

Quickly, she removed an unmarked yellow file folder from the drawer, opened it and stared in shock.

The folder contained five more notes—death threats—against the entire Rothchild family.

Notes her father had *not* given to the police.

These were not typed, either, like the first threat. They'd been created from letters cut from magazines and newspapers. Jenna was careful not to touch them as she read the words, horrified.

Whoever had crafted and sent these was threatening to systematically kill off Rothchild "trash," eliminating family members one by one after Candace. Each of the notes was dated, and every one alluded to the infamous Tears of the Quetzal, in increasing detail. And all five spoke of an old deed that needed to be avenged.

The last one was even signed, The Avenger.

A shudder washed over her as the rain lashed against the windows again, and fronds swished against the panes.

Why was her dad hiding these?

Had he kept these notes even from Natalie, her LVMPD sister and Candace's twin? Just as Jenna herself hadn't told anyone, including Nat, that she'd been to visit her sister the night of the murder?

Jenna was really afraid now. She needed to come clean, tell Lex everything that had happened the night of Candace's death.

And she needed to inform him about the existence of these notes.

But that would mean betraying her father. Maybe Harold had good reason to have withheld these from the cops. Maybe these notes weren't even from the killer—they were a completely different style to the first one.

She needed to speak to her dad, find a way to broach the subject of the death threats, and she'd make her decision from there. But as Jenna closed the file the headlights of a car swept up the driveway, and she heard the distinct crackle of tires approaching on wet driveway. She glanced up. She had to get out of here, fast. Quickly shoving the file back into the drawer, she closed it and flipped off the light.

Jenna couldn't face her father now…she needed to think.

Rebecca Lynn had set her up to find these. Why? And how had Rebecca Lynn known about them in the first place? Had Harold told Rebecca Lynn himself? And, if so, why not tell the rest of the family? Her stepmother had succeeded in her goal tonight—she'd driven a needle of mistrust into Jenna. Mistrust of her own father.

Carefully shutting his office door, she made her way quickly through the living room and up the marble stairs. She reached the landing just as the front door opened.

Heart thudding, Jenna peered down over the banister, saw her dad's distinguished silver head. And with a sick feeling, Jenna knew. She just knew that she was going to be forced right up against the fence, and she was going to have to pick a side.

The side of her family, a place of murky allegiances and mixed-up love, a place she'd always felt secure, the only place she'd ever really known.

Or the side of law—Lex's side.

Chapter 7

It was late Sunday afternoon, and both Lex and Rita Perez were still in the FBI office. Perez was meticulously combing through public records of Rothchild real estate dealings, putting together a detailed timeline of transactions. She was looking, in particular, for links between Harold and Frank Epstein's old cartel. Lex, on the other hand, was focusing on Frank Epstein himself.

The two families seemed to be intersecting in relation to himself and to this case, and Lex didn't believe in coincidence.

He was finding it tough to accept Mercedes Epstein had shown up at Jenna's auction, uninvited, and started a bidding war on him purely by chance. Or was he just trying to read too much into it all because Mercedes had worked at the Frontline at the same time as his mother? And because Frank Epstein had been the one to both hire—and fire—Sara Duncan?

Lex rubbed his eyes and pinched the bridge of his nose. He was also troubled by the fortune-teller's allusion to his mother being connected to the old Vegas underworld. Or was he also giving too much weight to the Lucky Lady's strange words?

There was no doubt in most minds that Frank Epstein did once have ties to the Chicago mob and subsequently to organized crime in Las Vegas. Epstein, now in his seventies, would have been in his late twenties in the late 1950s—a time when gangsters still owned and ran all the big Vegas joints. Epstein was reputed to have had a sharp eye for a deal, even at a very young age, and he'd made connections and climbed fast, eventually forming a powerful business cartel that had bought the old Frontline Casino. It was a mob-owned, Chicago-based union pension fund that had enabled Epstein to finance the razing of the Frontline and the subsequent construction of his massive Desert Lion—the sheer scope of his new casino unprecedented at the time.

Those were the days when no bank or legitimate investor would've come near the gambling business. Without mob money, the Vegas boom would have never happened. They were the days before Howard Hughes had started investing massive proceeds from his airline sale into Vegas property, giving gambling its first positive image, opening the doors to corporate ownership of hotel-casinos. After Hughes, Wall Street investors had finally sat up and started taking notice—and gambling had become acceptable to mainstream America. It was about that time that the federal government had started a massive crackdown on organized crime in Las Vegas, running most of the old gangsters out of town.

Epstein, however, had managed to elude the dragnet. He'd given the feds nothing they could pin on him. But they'd continued to watch him. They'd kept files on him, looking, in particular, to connect him with some of the brutal murders alleged to have been carried out by a man named Tony Ciccone.

A mob enforcer.

Lex continued to scroll down through the old microfiche files the FBI had compiled on Epstein dating back to the 1970s, noting that Epstein had hired Ciccone from Chicago to handle security at the Frontline.

He sat back, reached absently for his coffee mug, sipped. It was cold. He pulled a face, shoved the mug aside, thinking that one needed to understand the context of Vegas at the time. It was a period when the mob literally ruled Sin City. And people like Ciccone—who took orders from men like Epstein—commonly got away with murder. Murder and gangsters even added to the edgy glamour and allure that was Las Vegas in that era.

But when Ciccone had eventually come under investigation for a run of increasingly violent homicides, Epstein seemed to have severed ties with him. Lex scrolled further through the files, noting it was around this same time that some sort of rivalry had developed between Ciccone and Epstein. And Ciccone had broken away from Epstein, forming his own camp, and allegedly muscling into Epstein's business, on Epstein's turf.

It was also around this period that Lex's mother had been murdered.

Lex rubbed his brow. Was he insane for even thinking along these lines? What on earth could Sara Duncan have had to do with any of these people? The fortune-teller's words snaked back into his mind. *"Everyone was touched by those tendrils of evil. Everyone…"*

He shook off the thought, turned back to the files.

Apparently, before the feds had been able to pin the homicides on Ciccone, the Italian-American had simply vanished. Dematerialized into the ether. The FBI had mounted one of the country's biggest manhunts for the violent mob enforcer, but no one ever found a clue what had happened to him. It remained an unsolved mystery to this day.

And from the point of Ciccone's disappearance, Frank

Epstein's business seemed to have suddenly gone squeaky clean, Epstein apparently transitioning seamlessly into the new corporate era of Las Vegas.

The new Vegas has risen...

However, the FBI files on Epstein had remained open, and the feds continued to keep him in their sight. Now, decades later, the U.S. Securities and Exchange Commission, and the FBI's financial crimes unit, finally had a small lead on Epstein's alleged involvement in a massive junk bond scam. And now an undercover investigation into some of Epstein's other holdings and New York Stock Exchange transactions was currently under way.

Lex reached for his coffee, almost taking another swallow before he recalled how cold it was. He set the mug back down, turned to Perez. "You got any idea yet when exactly Harold and Frank were on good business terms, and when things went sour between them?"

Perez flipped through her notebook. "I got here that in the early 1980s, they were still in business. Seems things went sideways in the mid-80s when they dissolved a formal partnership."

"Does the dissolution revolve around any deal in particular?"

"Still looking into that."

Lex chewed on the inside of his cheek, thinking. Harold was a little younger than Epstein; still he'd been around and doing business in Las Vegas long enough to have been tainted by the organized crime that had once ruled Sin City.

"What are you thinking?" asked Perez.

About who could have killed my mother, and why.

"Just can't help wondering what happened to Tony Ciccone, you know?"

Perez twisted her thick, dark hair round a pencil and made it into a bun, the pencil sticking out the top. She did that when she was getting tired and needed to keep focus. "You think Epstein had Ciccone whacked or something?"

Lex shrugged. "A lot of people apparently thought so at the time. Ciccone was in Epstein's employ, and when Ciccone started drawing too much federal heat to Epstein during the crackdown, it looks like Epstein tried to sideline him, send him back to Chicago. It appears Ciccone didn't want to go home. He dug in, started trying to muscle in on some of Epstein's Vegas business himself. Then, poof, suddenly he's gone." Lex snapped his fingers. "Just like that. And Epstein goes clean as a whistle."

Perez got up, stretched her back. "I'm beat. Want some food? I'm going to get takeout."

"Uh…yeah, sure. Did you manage to get those records on Mercedes Epstein I asked you about yesterday?"

Perez rummaged through the growing pile of papers on her desk, extracted a file. She slapped it down on Lex's desk, reached for her jacket. "Pizza or Chinese?"

"Whatever," Lex said, opening the file.

"Oh—" she stopped at the door "—that fire in South America, at Joseph Rothchild's old offices? No record of it."

"No surprise, either," Lex muttered as Perez left the room. But what Lex saw when he opened the file *did* come as a surprise—Mercedes was not her real name. It was a stage name.

She'd been born Mary Roberts and had officially changed her name when she'd arrived in Vegas and started dancing. And what Lex read next chased a strange shiver over his skin.

Mary Roberts, aka Mercedes Epstein, originally hailed from bluegrass country, a Kentucky girl who'd run away from home at the age of seventeen. In the file that Perez had compiled were copies of newspaper stories about a distraught couple searching for their missing teenage daughter. But it was the next line that had chilled Lex.

The city Mary Roberts hailed from was *Lexington,* Kentucky. He sat back, feeling vaguely shaky. Not many people had the name *Lexington.* Personally he didn't know one. This meant nothing, of course, just *another* coincidence that a woman who had bid a fortune on him hailed from Lexington, Kentucky, and that she was the wife of a one-time mob man who had sacked his mother for being pregnant with *him.* And that she shared Lex's passion for orphan-related charities.

He dragged his hand though his hair, cursed softly. Perhaps the Lucky Lady was right. Perhaps Las Vegas was rubbing off on him, and now he was starting to look for signs, for connections. For omens.

He thought again of The Tears of the Quetzal, of the legendary curse.

Of Jenna.

He shook it all off. Superstition was ludicrous. He was a cop. He dealt in cold hard facts. Logic.

Still, it felt weird. He felt off, and no matter how freaking nuts it all was, somehow it *was* all dovetailing. On impulse, he grabbed the phone, dialed the FBI's financial crimes unit in New York, asked to speak to someone on the Epstein investigation.

It was late Sunday evening and Harold was still holed up in his study. Jenna paced impatiently outside her father's door. She'd been trying to find an opportunity to speak to him all day, and now she was dressed up and due at Cassie's big birthday bash being held at the Desert Lion.

But she couldn't go without speaking to her dad first. She just could not leave this for another day. She stopped outside his door, sucked in her breath, knocked. Harold detested being bothered in his study.

Jenna waited impatiently, getting tense. She rapped again, harder.

"What is it?" her father barked from inside.

She opened the door. The lights were dimmed, and Harold

Rothchild was sitting in his great leather chair with his back to her, feet up on an ottoman, whiskey tumbler balanced on the arm rest, as he listened to female vocals with the clear voice of a bird. He did this sometimes when he was brainstorming a particularly thorny problem.

He glanced round. *"Jenna?"*

"I need to talk to you." She set her purse down, struggling suddenly for a way to broach the issue.

He studied her for a long moment. "Why don't you take a seat and—"

"I don't want to sit. I want the truth, Dad. You're hiding things from me, and I want to know why." She gestured in the direction of his desk drawer. "Why didn't you tell me about the additional death threats to our family? Why did you keep those other five notes from the police? And what's all that stuff about revenge for a past deed and The Tears of the Quetzal? What was it, *really,* Dad, that got Candace killed?"

His face, usually so controlled, his blue eyes usually so deceptively friendly, suddenly turned dark and thunderous.

A warning to be cautious whispered through Jenna. She'd intended to broach the issue delicately, but she'd already botched it in her frustration. And she could see her father had already had a couple of Scotches. It was at times like this, loosened by alcohol, that Harold could get mean, and she'd become a little afraid of him, even though she loved him so much. Because of his power to hurt and reject her.

Because of her own need to be loved.

All those old childish emotions suddenly began twisting into a thorny braid in Jenna's chest now.

"You saw the notes?" he asked quietly.

"I saw them," she said. "Why did you hide them, Dad?"

He said nothing.

Anger began to bubble deep in her gut, fueled by her conflicting emotions. Jenna tried to keep her cool, but control was elusive. "Candace died, Dad—she was *murdered.* And those notes threaten our entire family with the same fate. That includes *me.* But you didn't think to let me know, did you? Oh no, the great Harold Rothchild is immune from death threats. Little Jenna doesn't need to know anything. Just use her to play with the FBI agent and mess up his homicide investigation so it can all be thrown out of court later—"

"Jenna, that's not—"

"Not true? Why should I believe a thing you say now? I think Lex was right—I think you *do* want to use me to obfuscate this whole business." Her heart was racing, moisture now filling her eyes. "Why? Why are you doing this? Why do you not want the police to solve this thing? Why are you putting us all in danger?"

He swung his feet down off the ottoman, took a deep slug of his drink, set it down and glared at her. "What were you doing in my office?"

"Is *that* all you care about?"

"What—" he repeated, cold and slow "—were you doing in my office?"

"The…door was open and so was the desk drawer—"

He got swiftly to his feet. Even in her four-inch heels, Harold positively towered over Jenna. She instinctively cringed inside but refused to take a step back. "Rebecca Lynn had been in here, Dad. *She* left the door ajar, and she left that top drawer open with the file sticking out."

A fleeting unreadable look shadowed his features.

"Rebecca Lynn knew about those death threats, Dad, and she purposefully set me up to see them." Jenna wasn't going to mince things now. She wanted to poke at him, about Rebecca Lynn, about everything.

Harold regarded her for a long moment, as if trying to control his rage before he spoke again. Jenna felt Napoleon nudge against her ankles, but she resisted the powerful urge to scoop up her little dog, hold him tight. Instead she met her father's glare head-on.

"They're idle threats, Jenna." He watched her eyes carefully as he spoke. "They're simply designed to unnerve us. My belief is that someone read in the papers about Candace, the ring, the legendary curse and just wanted to jump in on the whole Rothchild media circus. I will *not* allow the sender of the notes that pleasure."

"Is that not a conclusion the FBI should be making?"

"Does this mean you're going to tell your FBI agent about this?" His voice was ominously quiet.

"Why shouldn't I?"

He picked up his glass, walked over to his private bar, uncapped his bottle of prized whiskey, poured a glass—neat, no ice—turned back to face her. "Jenna, for all I know, Rebecca Lynn could have left those notes herself."

"Excuse me?"

"We're having…relationship issues. Rebecca Lynn wants attention. She could have done this to get it. Those notes you saw are clearly different from the first one, and the fact Rebecca Lynn showed them to you would seem to confirm my suspicions. You see? I kept those notes secret, therefore Rebecca Lynn did not get the attention she was seeking, and now she wants you to cause a fuss with me." He sipped his drink. "She wants to drive a wedge between you and I, sweetheart."

"So…you didn't speak to Rebecca Lynn about them at all?"

"No."

Jenna brushed her hand over her hair, suddenly unsure. "I…I still think this is something for the FBI to decide."

"Absolutely not. I will not have them messing around in my personal issues. Can you just imagine the media finding out my own wife left me death threats? I don't want the feds looking into my business dealings, either. Candace's murder has nothing to do with all that. It'll just cause trouble." He paused. "Untold trouble. Look, Jenna, you're not naive. Some of my dealings, like those with the Schaeffers, were not exactly kosher. An investigation into my private business could bring us *all* down, the entire Rothchild empire."

"Maybe it was Frank Epstein who sent the notes," Jenna said, pushing. "Maybe Lex was right, and bad business blood had Epstein wanting to avenge some old deed." She took a step closer to her father. "You don't want the feds digging into your relations with Epstein, either. Why? Because of old mob ties?"

He stilled. The color of his eyes seemed to fade, flat and hard as ice.

"Epstein didn't do this. He had nothing to do with Candace."

"How do you know?"

"Trust me. I *know.*"

She frowned. "What exactly—" she said, taking another step toward her father "—happened in the past with Frank Epstein, Dad? What makes you so darn sure about him now?"

Harold's neck corded, and a hint of nervousness seemed to flicker through his features. Which scared Jenna.

"You—" he pointed with his index finger off his whiskey tumbler "—have to understand, Jenna Jayne, that messing around with that FBI agent, leading him to look into Rothchild business dealings is going to end up bad news."

"You," she said, meeting his pointed glare, "were the one who set me up to get involved with Lex Duncan in the first place."

"Solely for information about the ring."

Again, the ring.

"You set me up to seduce him, Dad."

"Not be seduced *by* him," he snapped.

"Oh, like you can control the whole damn world! My emotions to boot."

He set his glass down slowly, seriously registering for the

first time that his daughter might actually have some real and very dangerous personal allegiances with the federal agent. His daughter was falling for the cop who could take him down. *If* she let him.

"It's gone too far with him, Jenna. End it."

She swallowed, shaking inside with fury. "You don't control me," she whispered. "You don't tell me to switch my feelings on and off at your own whim, for your own personal gain."

"Pick a side, Jenna Jayne. Choose your family, everything we own, or pick that man—a blue-collar federal agent," he spat the words out derisively. "For what? One night of hot sex, for the novelty of sleeping with a law enforcement officer?"

"No," she whispered. "For something *real,* Dad."

"Consider your actions very, very carefully, Jenna Jayne."

"Oh, I am."

"Consider, too, that your agent friend might know that you went to visit Candace the night of her murder and that he may have pegged you as a suspect, too."

Shock rocketed through her. "Rebecca Lynn told you?" she whispered.

He said nothing.

Hatred rustled like an ugly thing under Jenna's skin. Rebecca Lynn wasn't just trying to drive a wedge between her and her father; she wanted to see Jenna go down.

A very dark and dangerous thought occurred to her—was Rebecca Lynn crazy enough to commit murder? Could she actually be behind all of this?

"Special Agent Lex Duncan is using you, Jenna. Once he is through, you will be left with nothing, because you will have alienated *me.*"

"Is that a threat, Dad?"

He glared at her for several beats. "No, Jenna. That's a fact."

Chapter 8

Vibrating with anger, Jenna got into her car. "Damn him," she muttered to Napoleon, who was sitting in the passenger seat on buttery leather. She slammed her hand down on the dash. "How could my *own father* threaten me like that?" Jenna clenched her teeth, turned on the ignition, setting her convertible engine to a smooth, low growl. She didn't want to feel hurt. Vulnerable.

For the first time in her twenty-five years of life she wasn't going to give in to her dad, to her own subterranean need for her father's affection.

But that meant she was alone.

She should go find Lex, tell him everything. She should let him know that she'd gone to Candace's apartment that night to try and talk her impossible sister into a rehab program—if not for her own sake, for the sake of her two toddler sons. But Candace had wanted nothing of it. Sky-high on a cocktail of drinks and drugs, she'd launched a Ming vase at Jenna's head.

And yes, Jenna had cut her finger picking up the pieces. It had bled pretty badly. Her blood very likely had been left at the scene. Rebecca Lynn might be right. Perhaps Lex *was* spending time with her solely to glean information that could secure him a warrant for her DNA, or something, so he could match her to the blood. Jenna didn't want to deal with that thought right now.

She'd tackle it all tomorrow, because right at this moment, she was falling into her tried and true coping mechanism. And she knew it. She inhaled deeply, glanced at Napoleon. "Ready, Naps? Because we're going to partay. We're going to the Desert Lion, and we're going to make sure Cassie has the best damn birthday celebration of her life."

And with that, she drove out of the garage, the automatic door sliding smoothly shut behind her. As Jenna headed down the driveway she registered in the back of her mind that Rebecca Lynn's slate-gray BMW hadn't been parked in its spot in the garage.

Daddy's little trophy bitch was out.

She shoved ugly thoughts of violence toward Rebecca Lynn from her mind. The night was clear, the moon high and she was going back to the twenty-four hour buzz that was Las Vegas. Where she felt safe. Where she felt herself. Where the lights and the laughter and the frenetic pace spelled freedom.

And as she neared the metropolis, the dusky gold glow of Sin City shimmered like a beckoning halo in the hot desert night, and Jenna felt her spirits lift.

She didn't notice the dark sedan that pulled out of the shadows and followed her into town.

Cassie's birthday celebration was a glittering event that had attracted the A-list of young Vegas natives, along with special guests and family who had been flown in from around the country. The party was being hosted at the Desert Lion, Frank

Epstein's massive temple to excess, because Cassie's uncle was a friend of the Epsteins, and Frank was generously returning a favor.

But no matter how she tried, Jenna could not put her heart into having fun. Her champagne martini sat untouched on the bar, and Napoleon, perched on the stool beside her, glowered at the crowds from the security of his little designer purse.

The fact Jenna was in Epstein's opulent establishment didn't help her mood. All she could think of was Lex, his questions about Frank and her dad. Which in turn lodged thoughts of Lex himself fast and firm in her mind. And now Jenna couldn't shake the images of his body in the sun, or the memory of kissing him, his scent, the green sparkle in his eyes when he smiled. The way those eyes had looked so haunted when he'd heard about his mother from the Lucky Lady fortune-teller.

She wondered again about a possible connection between Sara Duncan and Mercedes Epstein. They'd have been roughly the same age when they'd both worked at the Frontline—Sara as a croupier, Mercedes as the leggy showgirl who'd won the hand and heart of the big Frontline boss himself. Jenna found herself scanning the crowds half expecting to see the sleek silver chignon of the elegant Vegas matriarch drifting by. That's what Mercedes did—she floated. It was those long legs. She must have been truly stunning in her day as a dancer. Jenna wondered what Lex's mother had looked like.

"Hey, hon, why so glum?" Cassie said as she came up to Jenna and Napoleon at the bar.

She sighed. "Just need to wind up I guess."

"Well, drink that martini, and you'll feel way more yourself." Concern tinged Cassie's bright hazel eyes. "Never known you not to sparkle at an event, Jenna. What's going on?"

Jenna couldn't even muster a grin. "I'm sorry, Cass. It's

just…this whole Candace thing not being solved. It has me…edgy."

Cassie crooked up her brow quizzically. "So, it's not going so well with Mr. Sexy FBI Agent, then?"

Too well.

"I really don't want to talk about it."

Cassie gave her a long and knowing look. "It backfired, didn't it? He's gotten to you."

Jenna said nothing.

Cassie threw back her head and laughed. "*The* Jenna Jayne Rothchild has fallen for a federal agent investigating her family for homicide."

"I fail to see the humor, Cass."

Her friend's smile sobered. "Come on, let's try our hand at blackjack. I feel lucky tonight."

Jenna slid onto a seat alongside her friend at the blackjack table and stacked a pile of chips on the green felt, but all she could think about was losing…her dad, the bedrock foundation of her life. Lex.

Jenna played her hand, flipped over her card. A bust. The dealer raked in her chips.

Frank Epstein pointed to the top left screen along a bank of monitors. "Take camera seven in closer. Zero in on the blackjack table."

The technician zoomed into the pit.

"There, see that woman in green at the table? Closer."

The image of the woman filled the screen. Frank's pulse quickened. He stepped forward, attention riveted by the beautiful young siren in a low-cut shimmering emerald-green gown. Dark hair fell in thick waves down her bare back, and her lush lips were painted a ruby-red, the precise shade of her nails. A red ruby pendant hung at her throat. Even the mutt's purse matched her outfit—emerald-green with little ruby-red accents.

Frank's security head, Roman Markowitz, came up beside him. "It's Jenna Rothchild," he said in his characteristic sandpapery voice, a result of damaged vocal chords in his youth.

Frank nodded slightly. So Harold's pretty young daughter was playing in his casino.

From the monitors in his Desert Lion security room, Frank could spy on nearly all activity in his establishment. Virtually every corner of his hotel was watched by these cameras—his eye-in-the-sky—including elevators. Select hotel rooms had also been outfitted with hidden cameras, which could be activated if necessary. Frank had gone so far as to install hidden filming devices in his own private penthouse where he lived with Mercedes, but those feeds only Frank could see, from a private setup in his office.

It wasn't that he was spying on his wife but he did like to record the activities of staff who serviced his penthouse. One never knew when a problem might arise and visual evidence could come in handy, perhaps even in a court case, for example. Information was currency in his business.

And in Vegas, everybody watched everyone else. 24/7.

Frank himself liked to spend several hours per day up here in the Desert Lion security room, mostly at this time of night when the action really started happening on his floors. And he never ceased to tire of the Vegas drama that unfolded nightly.

In one twenty-four hour period, at one of his blackjack tables alone, fortunes could be made and lost several times over. He'd see hearts broken, dreams shattered. People being seduced by luck and parted from their money by the shimmering illusion—the promise of a dream—that he was selling.

And all the while, he got richer.

Such was the game.

His security nerve hub was located adjacent to his private

office, and Frank felt that in standing up here, he was at the pulsing core of his happening hotel at the very heart of the Strip. Quite simply, he felt like a king.

Which, in many ways, he was.

It wasn't an accident years ago that his inner circle had started referring to him as the Vegas Lion, or Lion King. He held power most men could only dream of.

Harold Rothchild, however, was one man who had the wherewithal to take it all away. Harold remained one of those annoying, ever-present fault lines in the otherwise solid foundation of Frank's existence, a rival from Frank's past who had something on him—and on whom Frank had something in return. It was not a situation Frank liked to be in.

But he also couldn't simply make Harold go away—as much as he'd like to. He *could* kill Harold, but it would require some serious planning and risk. Frank was all about risk. Gambling, betting, odds—they were his business. Even so, the odds needed to be in his favor. The risk needed to be calculated, and resorting to murdering Harold definitely had the odds fully stacked against.

This was because Harold had "insurance," a videotape showing an illegal business transaction between Frank and himself. That tape was being held in a bank safety deposit box. It was evidence that would incriminate Epstein in a much broader range of illegal affairs and provide the FBI with the tools to start dismantling his entire empire. Harold had made it quite clear that should anything "untoward" happen to him, his will would ensure the tape was released into the custody of federal agents.

Epstein felt fairly secure that Harold would never take the video to the authorities prior to his own demise, because the tape would implicate Harold as well. Hence, keeping his rival alive was playing the best odds. For now.

Ciccone, of course, had wanted to eliminate Harold years ago—said he'd become a problem down the road. And Ciccone was right. He *had* become a problem. But when Ciccone had presented his plan to whack Harold Rothchild the climate in Vegas had already shifted, and simply offing people Ciccone-mob-style had come to hold serious consequences, especially during a period Frank was trying to get respectable for stock market investors. It became a time that Frank desperately needed to distance himself from Ciccone. But trying to hold the mob enforcer at arms' length hadn't been easy.

Frank had once liked Ciccone—but he'd have liked him even better with his hairy butt back in Chicago, doing the mob's union work. But Ciccone wouldn't leave Vegas. Instead, the stocky little Italian with a vile temper had accused Frank of betrayal, and he'd gone renegade, doing unnecessary violence as he'd tried to muscle in on Frank's turf. It turned into a bitter vendetta.

And things began to look real bad for Frank.

The feds had moved into Vegas in a big sweep to clean out Sin City and Ciccone was drawing serious heat to Frank—heat he didn't need.

Turns out, he didn't have to worry.

Ciccone "disappeared."

He'd been whacked, and Frank knew who'd done it.

"Rothchild's daughter is seeing the FBI agent assigned to the Rothchild homicide case," Markowitz rasped as he studied the gorgeous young woman down at the blackjack table. "He's the same guy Mercedes bid on at that auction."

Frank nodded slowly. He knew his wife had bid fiercely on Special Agent Lexington Duncan. He also knew why. He knew a lot of things that his wife didn't know that he knew. He was appraised of Mercedes's illness, too. It burned Frank, to think she was dying and hiding it from him. He loved her more than anything. For Mercedes, he'd literally move mountains.

He'd kill people.

"Could get interesting," Frank said, eyes fixed on Jenna. He wondered what game she was playing with the federal agent, how Harold might possibly be involved and how it could all potentially backfire on him—or Mercedes.

"Put a tail on her," he told Markowitz. "I want to know what she's up to. Get photographic records, anything that shows her and the federal agent in a compromising position."

One could never underestimate how useful those could be.

Frank and his security head exited the room together. "Did you take care of that fortune-teller at the Lucky Lady?" Frank asked quietly as they walked toward the elevators.

"Accomplished," rasped the security head, inserting his elevator card and keying in his code. "But Agent Duncan had already been there."

Frank's temperature rose slightly. "How do you know?"

"We made her talk first."

"She tell him anything?"

"Nothing that will bring him here."

They entered the elevator. Frank watched lights flicking down from floor to floor. As fast as he was moving to plug up holes, the past still seemed to be seeping up into the present, somehow triggered by that Candace Rothchild murder.

Frank for one wouldn't mind knowing who had killed the rich slut. She'd had it coming—that didn't concern him. What did concern him was the way it was filtering into his life.

He didn't like it.

Not one bit.

He clasped his hands behind his back as the elevator descended to the casino floor level, flexing his fingers in controlled irritation. This could not touch Mercedes. Not now. Not ever.

Especially when she had so little time left.

Jenna left the party at the Desert Lion early, looking forward to a hot bath and mind-numbing sleep. As she drove she was, as usual, grateful for Napoleon's company. She reached over and scratched his head fondly. A pet had always been the one constant in her life. Perhaps her only true friend.

"There's nothing like a pooch, you know, boy?" she told him. "No judgment, no worries if your hair looks like crap, just pure unadulterated love, and respect—" she hesitated as errant headlights from a car suddenly blinded her in the rearview mirror. The dark sedan behind her was coming a tad too close for comfort.

Jenna sped up a little, but the sedan kept pace. A cool sense of unease trickled through her. She didn't like the way the driver kept his brights aimed high. She changed lanes, weaving deftly between a big SUV and a delivery truck in an effort to avoid him. The dark vehicle swerved after her.

Was it *following* her?

Panic whispered through Jenna.

She recalled the warning notes in her father's desk drawer…*eliminating Rothchild trash, one by one.* She glanced up, trying to determine the model of the vehicle, but all she could make out was that it was a dark sedan.

The headlights loomed closer again, high beams blazing into her rearview mirror, making her eyes water. Jenna tightened her hands on the wheel. She saw an off-ramp looming ahead. It led off the freeway. On instinct, she swerved down onto the ramp, praying that the car would not follow, that she was just imagining it was tailing her.

It swerved after her.

The first dark tendrils of terror clawed through her. She *was* being pursued. The road fed into a quieter, secluded community near the deserted desert fringe. The sedan sped up behind her. Jenna's heart began to pound.

"Hold on, Naps," she whispered, hitting the gas, causing her tires to skid as she wheeled sharply round a corner.

But the sedan kept pace. The streets grew darker, more empty. Narrower. Raw fear tightened her throat. "What does that freaking idiot want with us?" she whispered to Napoleon.

As she headed over a long bridge, the headlights began to loom closer again. With one hand fisted on the wheel, eyes fixed on the road, Jenna groped under the dash for her purse. She pulled out her phone, began to dial, but the sedan drew up suddenly and smacked her bumper from behind. Her car lurched violently forward. She gasped, dropping her phone, as she clutched at the wheel with both hands.

It hit again, more at an angle.

This time her car slammed against the bridge railing on the passenger side, metal sparking against metal, tires screeching. She bounced back into the lane, swerving, managing to re-steady her vehicle, heart slamming in her throat, her body wet with perspiration. She saw the dark sedan speeding up again and veering wide out to her left, coming in for a sideswipe on the driver's side.

Oh, God, he was going to try and push her over the bridge railing!

She saw a highway on-ramp up ahead. She *had* to get back onto that freeway, where there were more cars, people. She gritted her teeth, punching down on the gas just as the sedan smacked sideways into her. She bounced off a median, swerving violently back onto the road. She was almost to the on-ramp, *almost!*

Jenna flattened the accelerator to the floor, screeching up the on-ramp as the sedan closed the distance gap at incredible speed behind her. It drew almost level with her as the road narrowed, forcing her vehicle to scrape against the concrete abutment, throwing sparks.

The passenger window of the sedan slid down. Then she heard it, something thudding into her car. He was shooting at

her! Oh, dear God, *someone was trying to kill her!* Another
bullet sparked off metal.

Adrenaline dumped into her system, firing every synapse in
her body as she kept her foot flat on the gas, focusing dead
ahead where she wanted to go. And Jenna careered from the
on-ramp onto the highway, bouncing and shooting diagonally
across four lanes. Cars screeched everywhere, radiating out
from her, but she had her fists clamped on the wheel, and she
aimed for the gaps between vehicles. A small truck swerved
madly, narrowly missing Jenna. But in doing so it connected
the back bumper of an old station wagon, sending it into an
instant 360 degree spin behind her. Cars and trucks swerved
outward from the spinning station wagon, tires shrieking, horns
blaring…and she heard the sickening thud and crunches of
metal against metal. But she *couldn't* look back. She kept
speeding down the highway, hands fisted on her wheel, limbs
shaking, tears streaming down her face. Soon the sound of
sirens began to wail, coming at her along the highway from the
opposite direction.

She passed the flashing lights and the screaming fire engines
and ambulances.

Shaking violently now, mouth bone dry, her body drenched
with sweat, Jenna drove for the one solid thing—the one person
in her world who would know exactly what to do, how to keep
her safe. Even if he was using her.

She pulled up outside Lex's modest suburban house, relief
washing through her chest when she saw that his lights were
still on inside. Jenna cut the engine, glanced up into her
rearview mirror, saw nothing but empty street.

She peered out the side windows. It was dark, the shrubbery
and trees moving in a hot breeze. Ominously writhing shapes.
Jenna was convinced she could see malicious intent in every
shadow, in every movement. She was terrified that whoever had

murdered Candace, whoever had said that one by one, they would eliminate the Rothchild trash, was now trying to kill her. And even though the distance to Lex's door was short, she was too afraid to get out, cross the dark space.

"Are…are you okay, Naps?" she said on a harsh sob, reaching with trembling hands for her dog who was cowering on the floor. Napoleon made a small whine and climbed up into her lap, and Jenna began to cry, hard. She couldn't stay here, but she couldn't move, either.

The front door of Lex's house suddenly swung open. Warm gold light pooled out into the night, and the agent, dressed only in faded jeans, stepped barefoot onto his porch. Jenna scooped Napoleon up, rammed open her battered car door and bolted for his front door.

"Jenna?"

She hurled herself into his arms. Lex drew her quickly into his home, shutting the door to the night, and he just held her until she began to calm down. Jenna sobbed against his bare chest, clutching Napoleon, and not ever in her life had arms felt so warm, so welcome. So capably solid and protective.

So safe.

He titled her chin up, concern—real genuine care—softening his gorgeous green eyes. "Hey," he said softly. "What happened, Jenna? What's going on?"

"Some—someone just tried to kill me."

Chapter 9

Jenna cradled a mug of sweet tea in both hands, her face wan and hair disheveled, her mascara smudged. A band of tension strapped viselike across Lex's chest, and a quiet rage began to hum inside him.

She'd told him about being followed, the chase, the pileup on the freeway, and he'd called in her description of the dark sedan. Lex could not begin to articulate the relief he felt that she'd come through unscathed, save for a dark bruise forming on her left cheek where her face must have hit the driver's side window. He got up, wrapped some ice in a cloth. "Here," he said. "Hold this against your cheek. It'll keep the swelling down."

She took it from him, eyes dark vulnerable hollows. Her hands trembled. He'd wanted to take her to the emergency room. She was clearly in shock. But she'd refused. She did not want to leave his house or him.

He also wanted to get crime scene techs to look at her car—paint scrapes, bullet holes. She'd need to make a statement also.

Lex swallowed against the emotion burning his throat and took a seat on the couch opposite her. He was disturbed by the fierce power rising in his chest, the wave of protective compassion that threatened to overwhelm him when he touched her. Afraid of what was happening to him.

Geez, he even had little Groucho Marx eating cat food from a bowl in his kitchen. He scrubbed his hands over his face. It was almost 3:00 a.m. Neither of them had had any sleep.

"Why don't you take my bed, Jenna, get some sleep, and then I can take you down to the station in the morning so we can file a full report."

"Lex—"

"You need rest."

"Would…could you…just hold me?"

He stared at her, pulse racing, Quinn's words humming in his brain. *We'll plug it as a covert op, and the legal stuff will be in the clear as long as you keep your hands off her.*

"Please?"

He got up, sat beside her on the sofa and put his arm awkwardly around her shoulders. His body warmed. Her skin was so smooth. She cuddled down into the cushions and leaned into him, closing her eyes. A small tremor shuddered through her, as if she was finally letting go of something she'd been bottling inside. He tentatively touched her hair with his fingers. It was soft. He stroked it gently with his palm, his heart swelling painfully in his chest with a sensation alien to him. His eyes began to burn.

They sat like that for a long while, in silence. Groucho came in from the kitchen, glowered up at Lex with his beady black eyes and evil little line of jutting-out teeth, then promptly curled himself at his feet. Lex snorted. He figured he'd just sunk to a new kind of low. Mostly because he really didn't mind the dog sleeping at his feet. He was kinda cute, in his ugliness.

"I…I need to tell you something, Lex," Jenna whispered against his chest. "About my father."

Lex tensed slightly at the tone in her voice. "What about him?"

She sat up, nervously pushing a thick tangle of hair back from her face. "He…he's…" she got to her feet suddenly, began to pace, eyes filling with moisture.

Apprehension deepened. "Jenna, what is it?"

She stilled, faced him square. "He got five more death threats against our family."

Lex took a second to process. *"When?"*

"Over the past few months. He didn't tell the police."

"Why the hell not?"

"He doesn't think they're important. But I…I think whoever left those notes tried to kill me tonight."

Rage began to vibrate dangerously in Lex. "Why didn't you tell me this before, Jenna?" he said as calmly, quietly as he could. "This is absolutely relevant to what happened to you tonight."

"I *am* telling you. Now."

"What do these notes say?" Pressure built inside him like a cooker.

She exhaled shakily. "Have you got something stronger than tea?"

He got up, poured her a Scotch, handed it to her. She took a deep sip and exhaled slowly. "Whoever sent the notes is threatening to take out the 'Rothchild trash' one at a time, after Candace. All of the notes alluded to some historic deed that needed to be atoned for, and all mentioned The Tears of the Quetzal. The last one was signed *The Avenger.*"

"How do you know which was the last one? Were they dated?"

She nodded. "And made up of letters cut from magazines and newspapers, not like the first one that came right after

Candace was killed." She took another slug of her drink, her eyes watering and nose going pink as it went down. "Dad said they were just some hoax, someone trying to get in on the Rothchild media hype after Candace's death. He said Rebecca Lynn could even have left them, seeking attention. But I think that whatever is going down is tied to that diamond and something that happened a long time ago, maybe even in South America."

Cool anger directed at Harold Rothchild arrowed through Lex. The bastard had put his entire family in jeopardy by not reporting those death threats, by not coming clean on the provenance of the ring. Because now, more than ever, Lex was certain Harold knew exactly where that cursed stone had come from. By not putting all his cards on the table, Harold Rothchild had left law enforcement chasing shadows, possibly costing months in lost time hunting down a killer. He reached for his phone. "I need a warrant," he said, crisply. "I need those notes. And I want to see what else he's hiding."

Panic shot across Jenna's face. She grabbed his arm. "Lex—wait!"

"What for?"

She couldn't speak for a moment and looked terrified.

"Jenna? You're not afraid of your own father, are you? Do you realize what danger he put you in? You could have been killed."

She cast her eyes down. "I…I love him, Lex. He's my dad. He's…all I really have."

Lex stilled, seeing in Jenna something he hadn't noticed before—a vulnerable young woman. In spite of all her sophistication and seductive glitz, underneath it hid a beautiful, sensitive creature who'd been born into the rarefied air of the Rothchild empire, a woman who had zero exposure to the normal touchstones of life. A lonely woman, even, who'd armored herself with a bright, breezy smile and who sought self-validation through attracting men. A woman who needed—*depended*—on the love and goodwill of her tyrant sociopathic father.

And in turning to Lex, Jenna clearly felt she was betraying her own father—one of the most powerful men in Nevada. She'd come to Lex's home, and in a sense Lex could see she wasn't going to be able to go back to her casino castle after this. He put the handset back down.

She glanced up, and his heart clenched. "There's more Lex. I…I was at Candace's apartment the night she was killed."

"You were *what?*"

"I…" She dragged shaking hands through her hair. "I should've reported it, and I didn't."

"What are you trying to say, Jenna?"

"You didn't know I was there?"

"No."

"So you weren't playing me, trying to get more information? Maybe find a reason to get my DNA so you could match it to my blood at the scene."

"Your *blood?*"

"I…I cut my finger on a piece of the vase Candace threw at my head. It bled pretty badly."

He swore. "Sit. Tell me. Everything."

"Lex—"

"Now!" He was furious.

She sunk slowly down onto the sofa.

He waited, stomach knotted.

"I…I went to try and talk Candace into going to rehab that night, for her children's sake, for my little nephews. Those toddlers are—"

"Stick to the facts," he said crisply.

She swallowed. "Candace was high, drunk, whatever, and when I mentioned rehab, she flew into a blind rage. She hurled a Ming vase at me. It smashed against the coffee table, and I tried to pick up some of the pieces and cut my finger on one, and then she threatened me with a fire poker if I didn't leave at once. So I did."

He glared at her, a vein thrumming in his forehead. "And you didn't report this, why?"

"I didn't think her drug problems and my personal issues with my sister were relevant to the homicide, or to the media circus that ensued. I…I thought it was a robbery gone wrong."

"You *thought?*"

"You have to understand, Lex, that every time the press got hold of something Candace did, the whole sordid business was splashed all over the papers and picked up by trashy tabloids nationwide. And it was her two little children who were ultimately going to suffer. Not her. She didn't give a damn. I just wanted it all to stop. For *their* sakes. Growing up knowing their mother was brutally murdered is going to be bad enough, damn it!"

"Geez, Jenna, don't you see? That vase, that argument of yours, it impacted a homicide scene. How in the hell were crime scene techs to know that broken vase wasn't part of the brutal attack on your sister? What you held back from the police has helped obfuscate an already confounding investigation! Who do you people think you are? Above the law, or what?"

Her mouth flattened. "It was a mistake, okay? I'm really sorry. I thought the Vegas police would catch the killer quickly. I thought it was just someone after the diamond, and that her latest drug binges wouldn't need to come out. Then the longer it took to find her killer, the more complicated it became to even mention I was there. I…I started to get scared."

Lex swore, raked his hand through his hair. "What, Jenna, makes this any different from what your father did in withholding critical evidence? Don't you see? You're playing the *same* game. And how am I supposed to do *my* job when you deceive me, hamstring me like this, huh? What're you trying to do, make a mockery of what I do?"

"Lex, no, it's not like that—"

"What's it like then?"

She lurched up off the chair, two hot spots forming on her cheeks. "I'll tell you what it's like. I have just betrayed my father! What I've told you could take—"

"Hey, you hid evidence, also."

"Yes, I did. And in confessing to you, in telling you what my father has done, I could take my whole family down, including my innocent nephews. I have just alienated myself from everything I know, Lex. My father said if I told you about those notes I'd have nothing. If he finds out I have done this, I won't even be able to go home. Because he—" she jabbed her finger toward the window "—owns the roof over my head. He owns my job. He owns who I *am,* Lex, and I've turned my back on him, on it all. I am on your side, damn it! Can't you see? I *am* telling you this, and I'll do everything I can to help you catch that killer." Her voice caught, emotion filling her eyes.

"You're only telling me this because you were attacked, and now you're scared," he said bluntly. "Otherwise you'd have come forward earlier." *Like when I kissed you, like when you put your hand on my knee in the dark car...*

She slumped down into a chair, burying her hands into her face. "I was going to tell you before I was attacked, Lex. I had made a decision to come clean, about everything. I...I knew I had to pick a side." She glanced up slowly, tears, mascara streaking her face. "And I did. I picked your side," she said, her voice small.

His heart constricted sharply. He crouched down in front of her, tilted her face to his. "You picked the right side, Jenna," he said softly. "You did the right thing." She began to sob, and he gathered her into his arms. She felt so good, so right.

And she'd picked *him.*

Jenna had put herself in his hands, and no matter his conflict over her actions, Lex was determined to do right by her. To keep her safe. But what were the implications—for him, his case, his job? Could he risk involvement?

He closed his eyes. God, was it even remotely possible that she could be with him long-term, that he, the orphan son of a hooker-turned-croupier mother who'd been brutally murdered, could have some kind of future with this Las Vegas princess?

Would it be such a terrible mistake to even try?

Jenna slid her hand up the back of his neck and drew his mouth to hers. He felt her tongue against his lips, and his consciousness spiraled liked a wild, dizzying fairground ride, shades of red and darkness swirling behind his eyes as heat arrowed straight to his groin. He moved his mouth over her lips, parting them. They were wet, warm, salty with tears and the lingering notes of Scotch. She opened under him inviting, vulnerable. Lex's heart began to pound as he teased the inner seam of her lips with his tongue. She moaned softly, sinking herself back into the cushions, drawing him on top of her. Her emerald evening gown slipped sideways off her breast and Lex's breath clean stopped. He moved his mouth along the smooth column of her neck to the firm swell of her breast, and he teased her nipple, feeling it bead tight and hard under his tongue. It sent blood rushing between his legs, and he began to throb, hard, with exquisitely painful, urgent need.

Jenna pressed her body up into his, kissing him deeper, wrapping her arms around him, wanting him, enveloping him. Breathing hard, Lex pulled back. While he could.

While he had a shred of sanity left in his brain.

She looked up at him, her lips swollen from his kiss, eyes dazed.

"Jenna…this is…I mean…the case. I can't—"

She sat up, pulling the fabric of her dress back over her chest.

"I'm tired," she said simply. "I…I'm not thinking things through. I'm sorry."

Lex stared at her, his entire body, every damn molecule pounding a tattoo that said *take her, take her now, she wants you, she's yours…*

But he couldn't.

Not without removing himself from this investigation first. Not without thinking through the repercussions first, while he still could. Lex didn't want to hurt Jenna. And he did not want to deny Candace Rothchild justice by having this case tossed out of court because of his actions.

And Lord knew, he didn't want to mess up his own life. Again. He couldn't afford to lose his career.

He swore to himself. This was exactly what he'd been afraid of. *This* was what he'd been running from when he'd tried to dump her outside her mansion in the pouring rain.

"Come," he said, helping her up from the couch. "You take my bed, upstairs."

"What about you?"

He cleared his throat. "I'm going to work some things out down here."

Lex flipped off the bedroom light, hesitating at the door. She was asleep already, out almost the moment her head hit the pillow. And there she was, in her shimmering green dress. In his bed. Jenna Jayne Rothchild, the Vegas princess. His lips curved, his heart feeling a rushing expansive sensation. He couldn't abandon her now. She was going to be in for a rough ride when he went after her father. How in the hell was all that going to work out? *Yeah, bro, never mind thinking things through—you're already well and truly sunk.*

He closed the door with a soft snick, blew out a lungful of air and then went downstairs.

Snagging an ice-cold beer from the fridge, Lex went to sit out on his porch, the hot night air silky against his bare chest. He took a deep swallow from the bottle and exhaled slowly as alcohol crept through his body.

He put his head back, looked up at the sky—crystal clear and splattered with desert stars. A gentle warm wind rustled the leaves in his small garden. Lex felt alive, more alive than he had in years. He took another drink, and a small spark of excitement began to shimmer inside him. What if—after this all cleared up—they gave it their best shot? What if she really *did* want him? Long-term.

Or was she just turning to him now because he was in the right place at her time of need? Maybe once things calmed down she'd scoff at what she'd done, tire of her blue-collar federal agent. Move on. To bigger and brighter things. To men who moved easily in her social sphere.

Lex swore softly. He was a freaking nut job to think Jenna Rothchild was going to want the kind of life he could offer. What was he doing thinking of commitment, anyway? Most men he knew would sleep with the woman and be done with it.

Besides, he reminded himself, he'd tried this road before. The orphan in him had craved family—a real one of his own. But he'd chosen the wrong woman, a high-maintenance social climber who had zero time or respect for his charity and volunteer commitments. Toss in a life-consuming law enforcement career, and that was a recipe for disaster Lex had no intention of repeating again.

He snorted, took another swig of beer, feeling the soft explosion of bubbles in his mouth. He was a pretty big flake to even think of trying to make a family again. It was probably the furthest thing from Jenna's mind.

He drained his bottle, got up, paused as he heard something rustling in the foliage along the boundary of his yard. Lex narrowed his eyes, peering into dark shadows, the interplay of moonlight and shrubbery and soft wind toying with his mind. He couldn't see anything, yet he felt an uneasy sensation. He went inside, slid the glass door shut and locked it. Then he went upstairs to check on Jenna.

Jenna blinked into the darkness as she felt Lex enter the bedroom. The room was full of moving shadows shaped by pale beams of moonlight streaming through the slats of the blinds, the wind in the tree outside his bedroom window. He came to the bedside, sat beside her, his bare torso a powerful silhouette in the surreal interplay of light.

She felt his hand, warm, strong and gentle as he brushed her sleep-tangled hair back from her forehead. She was hot, had tossed the sheet off, her evening dress slipping off her breasts again. But she didn't move to cover herself up. She wanted him to see her.

Jenna closed her eyes, savoring the sensation of his touch, his care. Because that's what she felt—care. It was what she'd glimpsed, briefly, in his eyes. And all Jenna was certain of right now was that she wanted him. All of him. All the time.

He was the first real thing she'd ever truly known in her strange whacked-up life. Lex was putting her in touch with the self she'd lost so many years ago, and Jenna was finding that she wanted something deeper than her shallow, glittering existence.

She was prepared to give it up for a shot at making it work with Lex. A gamble, yes, but this was Vegas. And the odds were that if she won, it would be worth it.

He caressed the side of her face, his thumb gentle against her bruise. A small shiver tightened her nipples and angled down into her belly. Jenna ached to wrap her hot body around his hard one.

"You okay?" he whispered.

Jenna swallowed, almost hurting with need, exquisitely conscious of every part of her body. She sat up, slid the straps of her dress off her shoulders so that the shimmering fabric fell to her waist, her breasts feeling suddenly heavy, swollen under his scrutiny. "You tell me—" Jenna whispered, reaching for his hand "—if I'm okay." She guided his hand to her breast. Lex inhaled sharply as his skin connected with hers. He cupped her roughly, drawing her closer.

Kissing her hard, he opened her mouth, his tongue hungry, aggressive. Jenna's world spun. She grabbed his hand, moved it down her abdomen, sliding it beneath her dress so he could feel the small silk triangle of her G-string. He groaned softly, moved closer, kissing her deeper, the sensation of his hand more urgent, more firm. Jenna parted her legs. He moved the fabric of her G-string aside, and she felt his finger on bare skin. Hot. Delicious. She opened her legs wider.

"Jenna—" his voice was hoarse "—this is…"

But she held his hand firmly between her legs, parting her thighs, drawing his body down on top of hers, as she sunk back on the bed. "I want you, Lex…" she murmured against his lips, her mind blind to anything but the sensation of his weight on top of her, his hand against her.

He gave in with a small moan as he thrust his finger up into her. Jenna arched her hips up desperate for more.

He began to move his hand, sliding another finger into her, teasing her sensitive swollen nub with his thumb until a pressure began to build low in her chest, screaming for release. And Lex lost any last shred of control. His breathing ragged, he yanked her dress down over her hips, tearing her scrap of G-string aside as she fumbled urgently with his zipper, her tongue slicking and tangling with his.

He positioned himself between her legs, his knees opening her thighs wide, and with one sharp thrust, he was inside her.

Jenna gasped, arching her back as her body accommodated him, and she smiled against his mouth. "Mmm, that emcee sure wasn't kidding about your loaded weapon, agent," she murmured, moving her pelvis against his.

He watched the upstairs window from the bushes.

He knew they were in there. He'd seen their shadows against the blinds earlier, before the agent came outside to drink beer.

Probably screwing each other now.

The idea agitated him, made him hard. Hot.

It had taken him some time to get around the highway pileup she'd left in her wake. Bitch. He'd guessed she would run straight here, to her cop. Well, she got away this time.

He'd have to find another way now, be smarter. He grew even hotter, harder at the thought—because when he did get her, he was going to do a lot more than just kill her. He was going to have her just like that cop was probably doing her now.

Chapter 10

Jenna met his fervor, arching her pelvis to him as he thrust deep into her, heightening every nerve in his body, driving him higher, hotter, until she stiffened suddenly, then shattered around him with a cry, her nails digging into his back. It drove Lex past the point of restraint—he yanked her hips up hard against his, and released into her, his vision spiraling in a wild vortex of dark sensual pleasure as she wrapped her legs tight around him.

They lay hot in the moonlit shadows, tangled in sheets, entwined with each other, Lex going soft inside her. And in his heart he felt whole. At the same time, he knew he'd failed.

He'd allowed himself to be sucked over the cliff edge, and he was wildly free-falling. Because now that he'd done this, now that he'd made love to Jenna, he wanted more.

He wanted it all.

And that scared him. Because maybe she didn't.

The darkness turned to dawn, and the morning sun began to stream lemon-yellow through the blinds, another hot desert day dawning, and Lex had to get to work. He was going straight to talk to Quinn and have himself removed from this homicide investigation. Lex prayed it wasn't too late already, that he could still hide from Quinn, from prosecutors and defense lawyers down the road, what had transpired between him and Jenna Rothchild while he was still assigned to the case.

He'd tell Quinn he'd elicited information from Jenna about her father that would secure a warrant to search Harold Rothchild's estate and bring him in for further formal questioning. Quinn would be good with that.

And Lex would need to step back from Jenna for a while in order to maintain the charade.

But at the same time, she was going to need him. The road ahead was going to be real rough because she was going to be a witness to the fact her father was obstructing justice. Lex *couldn't* leave her alone now as much as he *had* to step away for the case to proceed successfully.

He cursed to himself.

Excusing himself from this high-profile homicide investigation was also going to be a career killer. That he'd have to swallow. But Jenna, he had no idea how to handle. He swore again—what in the hell had he done?

One choice was clear—the first move. Get reassigned.

"Jenna—"

She opened her eyes, smiled up at him, brown eyes twinkling. Sated, naked, warm and beautiful. In his bed, his home. And she'd sneaked her way right into his heart—jaded old fool that he was, Lex couldn't believe he was daring to hope.

"What is it, Lex?"

He was going to tell her he wanted to make a go of it. But suddenly anxiety wedged into his throat, and he didn't know how to say it all and felt like an ass. What if she really wasn't on the same page as him? Maybe she was too young for him, had too much life in front of her yet to commit to him. And how stupid it would sound to tell her he loved her after a few days. Who fell in love after a few days?

Seems he did.

He got up, wrapped a towel around his waist, sun already warm on his skin. "Want some breakfast?" was all he could think of to say.

Something shifted in her eyes. She watched him, as if waiting for him to say something more, deeper, something about what had transpired physically between them. Anything.

"I need to get dressed," he said, instead. "Got to get into the office." He wavered. "I make a good omelet—" But before he could complete the sentence, angry barking erupted from downstairs. They both looked at each other, shocked almost, to remember that Napoleon was still in the house. Jenna jerked up in the bed, pulling the sheet over herself. "Napoleon?" she called.

He growled and barked again. Jenna's eyes shot to Lex. "Someone's down there. Naps never barks like that unless something has spooked him."

Lex charged downstairs. Napoleon was growling and yipping along the glass door that looked out onto the porch. Lex took his weapon from his gun safe, slotted in a clip, chambered a round and slid the door open. He stepped barefoot onto the porch. Napoleon bulleted out at his feet, rushing over the grass to a line of trees and shrubs along the boundary. He started growling and snuffling exactly where Lex thought he'd heard something rustling the night before. Jenna appeared on the porch behind him, his robe wrapped around her. He motioned for her to get back inside quickly.

Lex made his way over the grass, crouched down and examined the soft dry soil under the trees. Prints. And they looked to have been made by a male, about a size eleven shoe. Someone had been standing here. Lex glanced back at the house.

Whoever had been lurking under this tree would've seen him on the porch last night. He needed to get someone to look at these prints. He dragged his hand over his hair. What was he going to say? That he'd been making love to Jenna Rothchild instead of bringing her in after the attack on her life last night?

God, he'd been a fool. This could have been her attacker, right here, watching.

Lex swore softly, made his way back over the grass to the house.

"What was it?" she asked, her eyes wide.

"Nothing."

"But Napoleon never—"

"I want you to get dressed, Jenna. Take some of my clothes. And I'm going to call Perez to come pick you up. She can take you in, help you file a report—"

"What about you?"

"I'm going to get myself off this case."

"What…do you mean?"

He took her shoulders. "Jenna, this is going to get real complicated between me and you. It appears your father not only withheld those death threats but he also lied about the fire at your grandfather's South American office. We're likely going to see him being charged for obstruction of justice at minimum. And depending on how this all plays out down the road, and what else we learn from him in questioning, you may end up being a witness for the prosecution—"

She blanched, reaching for the back of a chair, the implications—the full brunt of what she'd done—hitting her square in the harsh light of morning. She wiped her brow with the back of her wrist, shaking slightly. She was also perspiring, probably still in shock. Geez, he should never have slept with her. "Jenna, listen—"

She jerked out from under his touch. "Look, intellectually, I know this all has to happen, Lex. But…can you…maybe leave me out of it? I mean, get a warrant for those notes without naming me or letting him know I betrayed him?"

"I can't do that, Jenna."

Panic mounted in her face. "Lex, you have to, please. I told you everything. I came clean. I just don't want him to know I—"

"Do you realize what you are asking me to do? I'm a law enforcement agent, Jenna."

She grasped his hand. "*Please,* Lex. For me."

"Listen, we need you, Jenna. Your father is withholding serious evidence in connection with murder. What he did, what he hid from police, could have gotten you killed. For all we know, he's up to something that *did* get Candace killed. He needs to tell us what happened in the past, with that ring, or more people could get hurt. And we're going to need your testimony to do what we need to."

She looked nauseous. "And…and you're taking yourself off the case?"

"I must."

"So you're just handing me over to your partner, who will take me to talk to agents who don't know me, who don't understand me like you do? What are *they* going to do to me when they find out I was at Candace's place the night she was murdered? I told *you,* Lex, because I trust you. I need you on my side now."

"Jenna, this way I *can* be there for—"

She shook her head. "I was a total fool, wasn't I? You were using me, just like my dad and Rebecca Lynn said you were. You were baiting me, setting me up to betray my family."

"That's not true!"

"Isn't it?"

He hesitated. "Look, Jenna, it might have started out that way—"

She glared at him, then swore and made for the stairs.

"Jenna!" he called after her. "Can you honestly tell me you weren't setting me up at that bachelor auction? Can you swear your father had *nothing* to do with that?"

She wavered on the bottom stair but didn't turn around.

"See? We both *started* out on the wrong foot, Jenna. But things have changed."

"Have they really, Lex?" she said softly, turning to face him, her big dark eyes hollow. "Because the way I see it, you're still a cop first." And with that she disappeared up the stairs.

"Jenna!" Lex cursed, turned in a circle. Damn. He wanted to kick something. He'd wanted to say he thought he was falling in love with her, that the core reason he was taking himself off the case was so that he could distance himself from the homicide and give their relationship a living chance.

She came down the stairs wearing his oversize gym shorts and a large white T-shirt that swam on her. Her evening gown was bundled under her arm, and her fingers were hooked through the straps of her high-heel sandals. Napoleon scuttled at her bare feet as she marched straight for his front door.

He grabbed her arm, swung her around. "Where d'you think you're going?"

"Back where I belong. Where I should have stayed. The only godforsaken place I know!" She jerked free of his touch.

"You've got to wait."

"For what, *Perez?*" She yanked open his front door and stomped barefoot down his small driveway toward her beat-up sports car. She wrenched the door open, and Napoleon bounded onto the passenger seat.

Lex followed her to the car, wearing his towel. "Jenna! Stop!" He grasped her wrist.

"What? You going to arrest me now?" Her voice was cool, her eyes defiant.

"I will if you make me."

"I dare you," she whispered angrily. "I dare you to tell your Special Agent in Charge you were screwing me, instead of just pumping me for information. Because if you don't, I will. And I'll tell the papers, too. Don't think I'm afraid to do it, either. Got nothing to lose now, have I?"

He clamped his hand over her door, stopping her from getting in. Anger bubbled inside him. "So you got what you wanted, did you, Jenna? You bought me at your auction, seduced me. And now you're going to use it to screw my case—is that how it goes?"

Her eyes flickered, filling with moisture.

"Think about it," he said, voice low and controlled. "You go to the papers with this story and you'll be doing exactly what your were seeking to avoid when you didn't tell the police that you were at Candace's apartment. You will once again drag the media circus down on top of your family—a nice legacy for those little toddler nephews you were trying to protect. And you'll be dancing to your father's tune again. Because I will now bet my last chip that he set you up to do that auction. He *wants* this case to go down the tubes for some reason, and he's *using* you to do it, Jenna."

"Let go of my door."

"I can't let you drive. You're not thinking straight. You're still in shock, Jenna. You did the right thing in telling me about those notes. Now you've got to find the courage to see it through. You've crossed that line, and you said it yourself—there's no going back now."

Tears glimmered in her eyes.

"Look, Jenna I *know* you're scared." He lifted her chin gently, but she jerked away.

She shoved past him, got into her car, slammed the door and started the engine.

"Jenna, don't do this." He banged on her window. "Geez, I…love you," he yelled. "I want to make this work, damn it!"

Her eyes flared, her mouth opened slightly. She cursed at him and hit the gas. Fishtailing down his road.

Lex swore, kicked the curb, then rushed inside to grab his phone.

"Perez, it's Duncan. I need you to get someone on Jenna Rothchild's tail ASAP. She's heading home right now. No—" he hesitated, sliding further over to the dark side. "I don't want you to bring her in. Just have her followed, make sure whoever you put on her tail has backup on call. Don't leave her alone for one second, understand? I…" He slipped even deeper into gray ethical muck. "She was followed last night, and…she might lead us to our target. Or flush him out." He shut his eyes for a moment, praying he was doing the right thing.

"You want me to tail her myself?"

"No. I need you in the office. I'm coming in—I'll explain." He needed Perez to keep working the angles they'd started, and he was going to have to talk to Quinn.

Lex hung up, wondering how in the hell he'd gotten to this point. Perhaps he should've chased after Jenna himself. But she was so strung out it might have driven her to excess speed, and a dangerous accident involving not only her life but others. Once she was inside the Rothchild mansion, she should be safe with all Harold's security and an FBI agent at the bottom of the drive.

A chorus of yipping rose the instant Lex walked into the bullpen. "Shut the hell up, would you?"

"Feeling a little rough, are we, Duncan?"

"Did you get someone on Rothchild's tail?" he asked Perez, removing his jacket.

Concern showed in Rita Perez's eyes. She got up from her desk, came up to him, talking quietly. "What's going down, partner?"

"They're freaking idiots, that's what. Where's Quinn?" he said, noticing the door to his office was shut.

"He's in Washington, gone for two days. You going to tell me what's going down with Rothchild?"

Lex sighed and swore. His little chat with the boss was going to have to wait. He was going to have to remain on the case, status quo, for another forty-eight hours.

"What you want Quinn for?"

"Just needed to speak to him about something personal."

Perez put her hands on her hips. "What you need is to speak to me, partner. You need to tell me what the hell is going on between you and that Rothchild woman."

"Nothing is going on."

"Oh? Apart from the fact she was followed last night, caused a major highway pileup and you didn't bring her in?"

"Executive decision," he said crisply, pulling out his chair.

Her brow tweaked up, and she regarded him suspiciously. "Let's hope it's the right one. For your sake."

"Haven't you got some work to do, Perez?"

"Yeah. I got work. I'm just wondering if we're like, still a team here, you know?"

Lex grunted.

She remained, arms akimbo, looking at him.

"Look." He glanced around the office, lowered his voice. "I'll explain it all, I promise. Between you and me, I got myself messed up personally with this woman, and I need to get myself off this case. And I will as soon as Quinn gets back."

She studied him for a few beats. "You gonna be okay?"

"Yeah, as long as you quit hassling me and get off my back for a few minutes."

Perez sat at her desk, began busying herself irritably with

her computer, and Lex felt bad. Rita Perez had worked for the FBI for twenty years now, and she'd always been there for her partners. She had that kind of rep, never fussed about stuff like tenure, and who'd been where longer. She was one of the most decent, fair, equality-minded people he knew. And apart from the recent bachelor auction fiasco, he trusted her with his life. "Everything okay with your niece?" he muttered.

She glanced up, that dark all-knowing brow of hers crooking higher. "What? You want to be my friend now?"

"Whatever. Don't worry about it."

"Marisa is fine," she snapped. "Better than fine—she's got a new man in her life."

"Who?"

"Patrick Moore, an accountant and a really decent guy who came out of nowhere into her life. I'm happy for her. She's had a rough haul since her miscarriage. She's opening up her own nanny agency now."

"That's great, Perez. Tell her I'm happy for her." And he was, genuinely so.

Perez hesitated. "I'm having them both over for dinner next weekend. Want to come?"

"Thanks. Maybe I will. I—" The phone on his desk rang, and he snagged the receiver. "Special Agent Duncan," he barked.

It was his contact from the financial crimes unit in New York returning his earlier call. And what Lex heard next made him sit forward sharply.

The New York unit apparently now had an informer, a retired personal accountant of Frank Epstein's from the old Frontline days who'd kept copious copies of records—payroll, budgets, tax files, receipts—all because he feared he might one day need "insurance" against Epstein. And among those records was a mention of a business deal with Harold Rothchild.

"Can you fax those pages through, the ones that pertain to Rothchild?"

"It's just two pages—a copy of a letter from Epstein's desk to Rothchild, outlining the parameters of a pending partnership in a property deal. I'm sending them as we speak."

Lex walked over to the fax machine, phone still to his ear. "They're coming through now—" He stilled when he saw Epstein's letterhead inching out of the machine, his mind veering wildly off track and back into time. Because next to Frank Epstein's name was a little logo—a cartoon lion with a crown on its head. *The same logo Lex had seen on the bumper of the metallic-blue Cadillac that used to bring the brown envelope of cash to his mother's house in Reno each month.*

Heart thudding, Lex removed the fax, stared at the logo. "That little drawing—"

"It was Epstein's logo for a while, back in the day," said the New York agent. "It's on all his personal correspondence from that period. Apparently those in Epstein's inner circle used to call him the Vegas Lion, or the Lion King, a bit of egotistical motivation that led him to dub his next big casino project the Desert Lion."

Lex hung up, feeling light-headed.

"What was that?" asked Perez.

"FBI New York." He bit his lip, thinking.

"Do they have something on Harold and Epstein?" She came over to his desk. "What's the fax say?" she asked.

Lex reached for his jacket. "I need to pay Epstein a visit. I'm going to the Desert Lion."

She cursed. *"Duncan—"*

He held up his hand. "I promise, I'll explain. Later. But where I'm going now has nothing to do with this case. This is personal."

"What about the fax?"

"On my desk."

She glowered at him for several beats, then threw up her hands and muttered something in Spanish as he left.

Jenna stormed into the hallway, Napoleon's little doggie nails clicking on the marble behind her. She was insanely relieved no one appeared to be home. But as she headed for the stairs, aiming for a hot shower, and some serious thinking, she caught sight of the headline on one of the morning papers that Clive routinely placed on the hall table.

The main story and photo was of the big auto pileup on the freeway last night. Her mouth went dry. Jenna snagged the paper, quickly scanned the story.

Thank God, there was nothing about any deaths or terribly serious injuries. There was also no mention of who had caused the pileup. Yet. She flipped the page and read the continuation of the article, a smaller headline underneath the story suddenly snaring her attention. And her blood ran cold.

There'd been a murder.

The owner of the Lucky Lady, a fortune-teller named Marion Robb, was found early this morning, her throat slit.

Jenna folded the paper, numb. Afraid. Somehow everything was connecting, and she couldn't see the patterns. She climbed the stairs, mechanically going through the motions of showering, dressing, feeding Napoleon. But all she could think of was Lex, of what the Lucky Lady had told him about his mother, and how the fortune-teller had alluded to Vegas's dark mob past and Sara Duncan's possible involvement.

Sara's throat also had been slit.

Had that dark mob past finally caught up with the present in that murky psychic store that sold dreams?

Jenna thought of her own father and his possible ties to Epstein, and of the stories about Epstein's old links with Vegas Mafia. She thought of the death threats in her dad's drawer—how they promised to avenge a past deed, how they all referred to The Tears of the Quetzal and how Candace was the "first" to be taken out. How her dad had lied about the fire in South America.

Jenna sagged onto her bed, inhaling deeply. Lex was the one person in her life that remained a lighthouse through this maelstrom. And she'd run from him. She'd pushed him away.

And he'd said he loved her.

Her eyes misted.

She couldn't begin to articulate how messed up that made her feel. Being with him last night, having him make love to her in his bed, was like nothing she'd ever experienced. He'd made her feel whole. As if she'd come home somehow.

More home than she felt here in the Rothchild mansion now.

She angrily brushed away an errant tear.

She'd been overwhelmed by it all—along with the shock of almost being killed and by the gravity of what she must now do to her own father. To her family. But in truth, Jenna knew the course was the right one, and she had to find the courage to go through with it.

Candace was, after all, family, too. She needed justice, too.

Jenna wondered if Lex was even aware of the Lucky Lady's murder. It wouldn't be an FBI case, as far as she knew, so he might still be unaware. She needed to talk to him.

She dialed his cell phone, but it went straight to voice mail.

She tried his office number, again voice mail. Jenna walked to the window, looked down into their beautiful garden, their wealth visible, tangible. She thought of Lex, his orphans. His mother. His strong sense of allegiance. Honor.

Of course he couldn't lie about her finding the death threats—she'd basically asked Lex to go against everything he was. She needed to see him. Talk to him. *Now.*

She grabbed her keys off her dresser and ran down the stairs.

* * *

Perez found Jenna Rothchild in a small FBI waiting area, not looking at all like the Jenna Rothchild she knew. Sweet little dress, flat sandals, hair all loose and unstyled, no jewelry. Jenna had asked to see Lex, and Perez was vaguely amused by the idea that the tail she'd put on Jenna Rothchild this morning had been led right back to the FBI field office. It appealed to her twisted sense of humor. "Agent Duncan isn't in, Ms. Rothchild. I'm Agent Perez, his partner. Is there anything I can help you with?"

She got up, looking nervous.

"You okay, Ms. Rothchild?"

"I…I'm fine."

"You got a pretty bad bruise on your cheek there. Did someone hurt you?"

She swallowed, tensing, arousing Perez's veteran instincts. Something weird was up. First Duncan. Now this woman. Acting odd. They were in on something, and Perez had a feeling it was more than just sex. Perez would do anything for her partner, even if it meant crossing the line, just a little. Because that's what partners were for, right? They had each other's backs. And Rita Perez was sensing something deep under the surface here. Something not so good. Something that maybe involved the Desert Lion.

"I…walked into a door," she said, touching her bruise.

"Duncan says you were followed last night."

Rothchild's eyes flickered fast. She turned and looked as though she was about to hightail it out of the place, skittish as a damn deer. But then she wavered. "Is Lex maybe out investigating what happened with that psychic murder?"

"Psychic?"

"I…it's nothing. Thank you for seeing me." She spun and began to stride out the building.

"You want me to tell him you stopped by, Ms. Rothchild?" she called after her.

Jenna wavered, turned. "Could you tell me where he went instead?"

Perez chewed on the inside of her cheek, very curious now about a psychic, a little plot of her own hatching. "Yeah," she said suddenly. "He went to the Desert Lion to see Frank Epstein."

Jenna's eyes widened for a moment. "Thanks." And she was gone.

Perez returned quickly to her desk, snagged her phone and called the tail she had on Jenna. "Hey, you just cut a break, Savalas. I'm taking over your babysitting duties, okay?"

"All yours. Fill your boots, Perez."

"Hey, Savalas—" she said before she hung up "—you hear anything about a psychic being murdered?"

"It's an LVMPD case. Happened last night. A woman who owns the Lucky Lady psychic store had her throat slit. Guess she didn't see it coming." He chuckled at his own sick joke. "So much for being psychic."

Or lucky.

"Careful you don't choke on your lollipop there, Kojak." Perez hung up and made for her vehicle. If Duncan wasn't going to tell her what was up his butt, she'd find out herself.

"Men," she muttered. "They need a damn mother half the time."

Chapter 11

Frank Epstein was not in the building. Lex asked to see Mrs. Epstein instead. It was a personal visit, but he wanted results, so he showed his badge. The receptionist picked up the phone, spoke to Mercedes, then handed Lex a special key card and pointed to a private elevator on the far side of the bank of main elevators. "She's in the penthouse apartment, thirty-third floor. She'll be expecting you."

Lex watched the lights blink as the car climbed to the top of the luxurious five-diamond casino hotel thinking that the little Lion King logo circa three decades ago, stuck onto the bumper of the pale-blue Cadillac might mean nothing. Anyone could have put that sticker on his car—it didn't necessarily mean that the man who drove it worked for either the Frontline or Frank Epstein. Or had anything to do with killing his mother. And the man who regularly brought the money certainly had not been the one with the hairy hand and raspy voice.

But the sticker in conjunction with the fact that Sara Duncan did at one point work for Epstein, and then mysteriously packed her bags and left in the quiet of night for Reno after allegedly being sacked by Epstein, is what had now brought Lex here. He wanted to hear from Frank Epstein's mouth the circumstances around the firing of his mother. And in Epstein's absence, Lex planned to ask Mercedes flat out if she'd known Sara Duncan and who might have been visiting her in Reno once a month in a blue Cadillac convertible. With a brown envelope full of cash. And her husband's Lion King logo on his bumper.

The elevator car stopped on the twenty-ninth floor, and two suits got in. Both sported Desert Lion name tags. The older man's tag decreed him Roman Markowitz, security head. Lex judged him to be in his sixties, but still a powerful man with darkly tanned olive skin and a thick head of pepper-gray hair. He threw an odd glance at Lex, then pressed the button for the thirtieth floor. Hairy hands, Lex noted. The doors slid closed, and the car began to ride up again.

It stopped, and as the two men exited the car, the older one turned to the younger. "Should be a long night."

The blood in Lex's veins turned instantly to ice.

The voice!

The doors slid closed.

He stared at them in a moment of raw shock. He'd know that distinct sandpapery voice anywhere—a sound that had haunted his childhood dreams. And lived in his adult ones.

The voice of the man who'd killed his mother.

Lex lurched forward and punched the Open Door button, but it was too late. The car had started to climb again. He hit the button for the thirty-second floor instead. Pushing through the gap in the doors as they started to open, he dashed down the passage, twisting and turning through the mazelike layout, looking for fire exit stairs. He bashed through the fire exit door, an alarm going off as he clattered down two floors, hit the bar to open the door to the thirtieth floor. But his weight slammed solid up against the door. It was locked from the inside of the stairwell. A security measure.

He swore. Then he heard footfalls clattering down the fire escape stairs. He'd set off the alarm. They were probably watching him right now from the cameras up in the security room—the omnipresent Vegas eye-in-the-sky. Lex squared his shoulders, and pulling his jacket straight, he began to calmly climb back up the stairs. Two security men stopped him. "Excuse me, sir—"

Lex held up his badge. "I'm on my way up to see Mrs. Epstein. Looks like I must have gotten off on the wrong floor."

The security guards exchanged sharp glances.

"You can check with Mrs. Epstein's receptionist if you like, she's expecting me," he said casually as he pushed past them. "I'll just head back up the way I came."

As Lex went back through the fire door the guards had left propped open, he heard one of the men key his radio, checking Lex's story and clearing him with reception. He made for the private elevator, heart slamming.

He'd bet his life that the security head for the Desert Lion was the same man he'd glimpsed through the louvered slats of the closet, wielding the knife that had slit his mother's throat. The voice, skin tone, age, hair, his association and current position with Epstein's casino all fit.

And now he had a name—Roman Markowitz.

Lex wondered if Markowitz knew who he was—that Special Agent Lex Duncan was actually the child of Sara Duncan, the child he'd come looking for on that fateful day in Reno thirty years ago.

Even if Markowitz didn't know, Lex had little doubt he'd be watching him right now via the security camera in the elevator, especially after the little incident on the stairs. And he'd be checking Lex's credentials, asking himself why a federal agent was visiting Mercedes Epstein.

It occurred to Lex, as the elevator bell dinged on the penthouse floor, that either way, Markowitz probably felt safe. Because he had no idea that Lex had recognized him or even could. After all, Lex had not been able to describe his mother's assailant to the police all those years ago. All he had was the memory of a voice. But no one understood just how indelibly that distinct voice had been burned into his brain.

The doors slid open, and Lex stepped into the penthouse lobby.

A butler showed him into a living room with elevated ceilings and a massive wall of tinted glass that overlooked the Las Vegas Strip below. The decor was all done in shades of cream and white. Even the orchids were white, the only contrast being the glossy black Chinese vases that contained them, and the black granite bar in the corner.

Mercedes was standing at the windows, her back to him as Lex entered the room. She was dressed in cream as if to match her decor—a sleek image of matriarchal elegance.

"Lexington," she said, looking out the window. "I was hoping you'd come."

For a second Lex was at a loss for words. No one had called him Lexington since his mother—and then the Lucky Lady.

She turned slowly, smiled, holding out her hand. "It's so good to see you. Take a seat. Can I offer you something to drink?"

He ran his tongue over his teeth, stepped forward. "No, thank you. What do you mean you were hoping I'd come?"

"We have so very much to catch up on."

"I beg your pardon?"

She nodded. "I understand, it's confusing."

An unspecified tension tightened like a wire around his chest. "I came to see your husband, Mrs. Epstein. But Frank

Epstein was not available, so I was hoping you'd help me out by answering a few questions."

She raised her elegant brow. "Is it a federal matter?"

"A personal one."

She looked at him for a long time, something strange and unreadable in her features, something that made him real uneasy. "What is it that I can help you with?" she said finally.

"Did you once know a young woman, a croupier, by the name of Sara Duncan?" he asked. "She would have been working at the old Frontline Casino around the same time you were there."

Several beats of silence thickened the air.

"Please," she said, very quietly. "Will you sit?"

Lex glanced at the virginal cream sofa, the matching chairs. "I'd prefer to stand—this shouldn't take long." He didn't like the look in her eyes, the unease he was feeling. Something big was coming down the pike here, and he had no idea what it was.

She walked to the bar counter, moving smoothly on impossibly high heels. She reached for a bottle of mineral water, uncapped it. "I knew Sara," she said as she poured a glass. "What do you want to know about her?"

"She was my mother."

Mercedes put the glass to her painted lips, sipped slowly, eyes intent on his. She set the glass down, a small chink of crystal on the black granite surface of the counter. "No, she wasn't, Lexington."

"I...excuse me?"

"Sara Duncan was not your mother."

He stared at her blankly.

She inhaled. "I'd really prefer you to sit, Lexington."

"Right about now, I really don't want to sit."

She nodded, turned away from him, looked down on the activity on the Strip thirty-three stories below. "It's been such a long time, so much in between. A lifetime really." She paused. "I had a one-night stand, Lexington. Just over thirty-five years ago."

Roman Markowitz had called Frank Epstein immediately upon encountering Special Agent Duncan in the private elevator. Epstein's driver had rushed Frank back to his hotel. He now sat in his private viewing room, watching the video feed into his own penthouse apartment. Markowitz stood at his side.

"You think he recognized you?" said Epstein, eyes glued to the monitor.

"Not a chance. He has no idea who I am."

Epstein nodded his head. "Keep it that way."

"How do you want to play this?"

Epstein studied his beautiful wife. "Let's hear what she tells him and see how he reacts. We'll take it from there," he said quietly. "What happened the other night with the tail on the Rothchild heiress by the way?"

"We lost her in a car chase. Someone else was following her. Caused the freeway pileup."

"You see who it was following her?"

"Negative."

"Interesting," Epstein mused.

"What does your one-night stand have to do with Sara Duncan?" Lex wasn't sure he wanted to hear what was going to come out of Mercedes Epstein's mouth next.

She ignored his question. "It was a crazy, impulsive and very dangerous thing to do, because I had recently married Frank, and Frank was a very, very possessive man." She was quiet for a few seconds, staring down at the tiny cars far down in the street. "I'm sure you know the rumors about Frank in those days."

She spun round suddenly. "I fell pregnant that night, Lexington. And do you want to know what the irony is? The irony is that Frank has always been unable to sire children. As much as I needed to hide the affair, I couldn't even begin to think of passing off my baby as his. And I couldn't get rid of my unborn child. It was not in me to do so."

Nausea rose in Lex as the meaning behind her words burrowed into his brain. "Who…did you have this affair with? Who was the father of your child?" His voice came out hoarse.

"A man by the name of Tony Ciccone. He worked for Frank. He was—"

"I know who he was."

Pain twisted into her features, and her eyes glimmered. "Tony told me to get rid of the child. He said Frank would murder us both if he found out, and I believed him. But I could not go through with an abortion. I…" Her voice hitched. "I…I just couldn't."

Lex didn't trust himself to speak.

"So I arranged to go on an extended tour. I was a dancer back then, and Frank was very busy with a major project at the time and wanted to keep me happy. He'd have given me the world if he could. He has given me so much—"

"The baby?"

She moistened her lips, nodded. "I timed my tour so that I could carry my child to term, and I gave birth in secret, where Frank wouldn't find out."

"A boy."

"Yes," she said quietly. "And I named him Lexington." Her eyes misted over, and her voice grew thick. "I named him for my hometown in Kentucky because I had a desperate need to root my son with some part of myself, my history, before I had to give him away."

Lex ran his hands over his hair. Feeling hot. He needed air. He needed to get the hell out of this place. He didn't want to hear what he was hearing. Didn't want to believe it…couldn't process it. "I…I am that son."

She nodded. "I entrusted you to Sara Duncan's care."

"You *gave* me to Sara Duncan?"

"She was a good person, Lexington. And she needed the kind of money that Tony and I could give her to do this for us."

He closed his eyes for a moment. This woman was trying to tell him that he—a federal law enforcement agent—was the son of one of the most notorious and violent gangsters in the country? That *she* was his mother?

Right about now, he needed a drink. No, he needed to get blind freaking inebriated. He needed to smash something. Disbelief, anger—he couldn't even articulate what—was building like a Molotov cocktail inside him. But he remained rooted to the spot. It was like watching a train wreck, the train wreck of his life, and he couldn't tear himself away.

"Tony Ciccone is—"

"Your father."

He swore. Violently.

"Lexington, I know this must—"

He held up both hands, palms out, keeping her at bay, not wanting to hear more, yet compelled to stay and hear it all. "Just…just give me the facts, keep it simple."

She had the audacity to look hurt. "Tony went ballistic when he found out I refused to terminate my pregnancy. He had a terrible temper, and he was convinced Frank would tear him apart limb by limb with his bare hands. I was afraid of Frank, too. As much as I love him, he can be a fearful man when crossed. But I do love him, above all else—"

"Please, Mrs. Epstein." Lex couldn't even call her by her first name now. "The facts."

"We paid Sara handsomely to take you as a newborn and to register you as her own child in Reno. She feigned pregnancy while I was away on tour, making herself look progressively advanced. It was a policy of Frank's that no visibly pregnant women could work his casino floor, and Sara caused a scene over it, as we had planned, and got herself fired. She then left for Reno, where we delivered the baby to her."

"*The* baby," he said, almost inaudibly.

"You."

"And then?"

"And then Sara had enough money to buy herself a house and to raise you on her own. We continued to pay her a monthly stipend, cash, organized by Tony. Non-traceable, of course."

Apart from the pale-blue Cadillac that came like clockwork to their house. "Who brought her the cash each month?"

"Jackie Winston, a man in Tony's employ."

"Did this Jackie Winston work for Frank Epstein as well as run personal errands for Tony Ciccone?"

"Why do you ask?"

"Just answer the question."

"Yes, he did work for Frank, but Tony put Jackie on a separate payroll as well. Frank didn't know this. You see, Tony was trying to coax several of Frank's men over to his side at that time. Frank and Tony were in a battle over…certain things in their…business relationship."

That would explain the frontline logo on Winston's blue Cadillac. "Do you know who killed my mother, Mrs. Epstein?" He couldn't *not* think of Sara as his mother. As far as Lex was concerned, she was the beautiful young woman who had held him, loved him, laughed with him, praised him when he came home from school with good marks. Made his lunches, found Mr. Teddy when his bear got lost…held him tight when he was sad. He didn't give a rat's ass what anyone said—Sara Duncan *was* his mom. And no one was his father. Not as far as he was concerned.

"I don't know who killed her, Lex," she almost whispered. Fear, or some other emotion darkening her eyes and blanching her skin.

"Don't lie to me. Not now."

"All I can tell you, Lexington, is that it was one of Tony's henchmen who did it, one who routinely handled Tony's dirty—or as he called it—wet work."

The one with a raspy voice who was inside this casino hotel this very minute. Still alive and kicking while his mother had been stone-cold dead for thirty years.

She inhaled shakily. "The first I heard of Sara's death was when I opened the newspapers the morning after she was killed. I called Tony right away. As I mentioned, this was at a time when Frank and Tony were having a very serious falling out. Frank was insisting Tony return to Chicago, and Tony was refusing. It made for some very bad blood. Frank, however, had the upper hand…it's a long story, but Tony figured he was going to get leverage by sending someone to kidnap you, and he was going to hold you—and me—ransom to get me to twist Frank's arm. He said if I failed to change Frank's mind, he was going to deliver the kid—you—to Frank in person. You were going to be the living flesh and blood proof of my infidelity and how I'd cheated him all those years."

Mercedes took a deep swallow of water, and Lex noticed her hands were trembling. "It…it was a really foolish thing for Tony to do, but he was growing more and more irrational, and violent, and the excessive drinking and drugs he was taking didn't help." She hesitated, looked Lex directly in the eyes. "If you know who Tony Ciccone was, Lexington, as you say you do, then you'll know the history and the rumors that circulated around him. You will know what people say he did. Frank needed to distance himself from all that, because he ran a clean operation."

Like hell. Lex glared at her. "Go on."

"But the kidnapping went wrong. Sara apparently hid you and shot and injured Tony's man, and he fled when he heard the police coming."

"Did this…man survive his gunshot injury?" Lex asked, seeing in his mind a replay…the checkered pants, the man's hairy hands, the glint of the knife. His mother's blood.

"I don't know."

"You're not telling the truth."

"I have nothing I want to hide, Lexington. I am telling you this because I need to. I am ill—seriously ill—and the prognosis is grave. I might have only days left, weeks at the most. When things start to go wrong in my body, it will be fast. My husband doesn't know I am sick. He doesn't know any of what I am telling you."

"Then why *are* you telling me."

"I need to," she said simply. She walked across the room, almost took a seat on a white chair, but restrained herself from showing weakness. Instead she forced her spine straight again. A proud woman, no doubt, but now that Lex looked carefully, under it, he could see a frailty. Under her artfully applied makeup was a face that was pale. Sick.

"When you approach the end of life, Lexington, and you look back over all that you have done…I…I just need to make peace with my God." Her eyes glimmered again. "And to do this, I needed to see you, to look into the eyes of my son, and to tell you the truth. It's my atonement. My absolution. This one thing I must do before I pass from this world."

"So it's for your own satisfaction. Because it's clearly not for mine."

"The truth, Lexington, it sets one free."

"And this truth of your affair, what do you expect it will do to Frank?"

"You don't need to tell him," she stated.

"So the truth sets only certain people free?"

She said nothing.

Lex walked to the window, looked down at the city of sin and light. Of illusions, deception. Of promise, fate, fortune. And ruin.

"Will you tell him?" she asked very quietly.

"I'm a federal agent, Mrs. Epstein. You've just told me who is behind the unsolved murder of a woman. It's a thirty-year-old cold case that could now, finally, find its way to closure. Frank will become part of that investigation, given his alliances with Ciccone, and the fact he is your husband."

"Frank had nothing to do with Sara's murder."

"He did, Mrs. Epstein. He was the target of the kidnapping attempt that went wrong. He was the reason for it all."

"And who would you see prosecuted at the end of it?" she asked. "Exactly who would stand trial—a dead man?"

"Justice must be done."

"Tony Ciccone is *dead*, Lexington. Gone. There's no one to arrest, no one to try in court. No need to bring it all up."

"It never ceases to amaze me," Lex said slowly, "how the Epsteins, the Rothchilds, the Schaeffers of this world truly think the rules apply differently to them—that you're somehow above it all."

She glanced at the street way below. "We are above it, Lexington," she said softly. "It's the way the world works. Money is power. Especially if you know how to use it."

"Like Frank does."

"Yes, like my husband. And all you will do is hurt him if you tell him about my infidelity. And he has infinite—and I mean *infinite*—power to hurt you back."

"A threat?" Lex snorted derisively. "You have this desperate need to tell me that I am your son, to atone with your God, but you must threaten me at the same time?" He spun, strode toward the exit. "You people make me sick. Besides, you have no proof you are my mother. I have no reason to believe it."

"DNA will prove—"

"There's no way in hell I'm taking a DNA test to find out *you* are my mother." He stalked into the lobby, rammed the elevator button.

"Would it help if I told you where Tony Ciccone's body is?" she called out.

Lex froze. He turned slowly, stepped back into the living room. "How do you know where he is? Did Frank kill him?"

"I did. I shot and killed the father of my child."

Lex stared at her, heart pounding. "Why?"

"Because of what he did to Sara," she said, the steel returning to her eyes, her neck corded tense. "And because his henchman allowed you to witness the horror. Because he allowed *my son* to become an orphan. The remorse, the guilt, it has been horrific to bear. It's why I have always supported the Nevada Orphans Fund, Lexington. And until you left Reno, I always knew where you were. And then when I saw your name in the paper in connection with the Rothchild homicide case, I knew you'd come back to Nevada."

She inhaled deeply. "Then I saw your name on that bachelor auction list, and I…" Her voice faded and tears began to stream down her cheeks. "It's why I came to see you with my own eyes and why I bid on you that night. I pushed the bidding sky high because…because I couldn't stop myself. I wanted that young Rothchild heiress to know just how much my boy was worth, and I wanted the orphans fund to get as much of her cash as she could give."

Lex shook his head, staring at the woman who said she was his mother.

"You can't put a dollar value on a person, on a baby."

"This is Vegas, Lexington. People can buy what they like."

Including a fake mother.

"Where's Ciccone's body?" he said coolly. "What did you do to him?"

Mercedes steadied herself by reaching for the back of a chair. "When I read about Sara's murder in the paper, I phoned Tony right away, and I learned what he'd done. I set it up to meet him at a place in the desert, an isolated spot that Tony and I had been together before, a ghost town where they used to mine silver. I said I had something important to tell him about Frank, and that I was worried about being followed, so he had to be careful not to tell anyone or bring anyone. He trusted me, Lexington. Tony, in his way, adored me, and he had no idea just how much hatred he'd put into me. I shot him, out in that desert. I rolled his body down the mine shaft. He didn't see it coming."

The words of the Lucky Lady psychic sifted into his mind. *A past...death...buried in the Mojave sands...sands of time...death to be avenged...*

Lex tried to swallow, trying to absorb what she was telling him—that she knew the answer to a mystery that gripped the nation thirty years ago, that she had killed a notorious Vegas gangster...and that gangster was his father.

"Why should I believe this?"

"Because I'll tell you exactly in which mine shaft you will find Tony Ciccone's remains, if there's anything left of him."

"Then, Mrs. Epstein, I'll see that you are brought in and charged with homicide."

A sad smile curled over her mouth. "I very much doubt, Lexington, that I will live long enough to see that."

"Where's the body?"

"At a small ghost town thirty miles southwest of Vegas, down a shaft in the old Conair silver mine. There's a main headframe, easy to spot. Next to it is an old metal-sided building. If you go about two hundred yards east of that, you'll find another shaft opening covered with a metal grate. He's down there."

Lex studied her. This woman, this proud Vegas matriarch, an ex-showgirl, was supposed to be his mother and a cold-blooded murderer?

"Why'd you sleep with him, with Ciccone?"

"It was a wild time, Lexington. We were all young, flush with cash, liquor, drugs. We felt like gods. We *were* gods, in our world. Las Vegas was our oasis, our desert kingdom. And Tony was rough, sexy. He had an edge that women liked. You have his Mediterranean complexion—"

Lex shot up his hand. He didn't want to hear that he resembled Ciccone in any way whatsoever. "One thing I still don't understand is that you have so much to lose by telling me this. And so little to gain. Why? Why tell me at all? Maybe you'd have done me a favor keeping quiet."

She shook her head. "I don't think you'll ever understand just how much I have gained, Lexington. Looking at you, right here, in front of me, in my home. My *son.* Whom I have thought about every waking day for thirty-five years. It clean broke my heart, Lexington, to hand over that small, warm bundle the day I gave birth. I have never, ever felt so proud as when I bore you into this world. The sky had never looked brighter, and I had never grasped so keenly the meaning and sense of life." She wavered. "And I've never, ever felt so lonely, so hollow and empty, as when I had to place you into the hands of another woman."

Lex scrubbed his hand hard over his brow. Crap, this was a messy tangle of love, adultery, murder, and revenge—old Las Vegas mob-style. And the only reason he'd stumbled upon this dark and dirty truth about his own past was because Harold Rothchild's old connection with Frank Epstein had led him here.

"*...there are still people in town who will go to great lengths* *to ensure that the past stays where it belongs—buried. You go trying to mess with that, and you're looking to be messing with some real bad ghosts…"*

Yeah, well now he knew just how bad those ghosts really were.

"What is your illness?" he asked calmly.

"An advanced form of leukemia. When my system starts to fail, it will be very fast. And it could happen anytime. Today. Tomorrow, next week."

Lex stared at her for several beats, then turned and exited the penthouse without looking back, his heart stone-cold numb.

His soul empty.

Mechanically, he pressed the elevator button for the lobby and began the ride back to ground level.

He finally had one answer he'd been searching a lifetime for—he knew the name of his father. And he felt more alone than ever, more at a loss as to who he really was. Because in a way, he'd just lost his mother. He'd just lost everything he thought he'd ever known.

Empty, emotionless, alone, he exited the elevator.

And there she was—Jenna—pacing agitatedly in front of the elevators, wearing an innocent summer dress with a small floral print, flat sandals, loose-flowing hair. Her eyes lit brightly when she saw him, and she ran to him.

Lex took her in his arms, wrapped himself around her. Held tight. As tight as he dared without hurting her. She was suddenly a buffer against the overwhelming emotion threatening to crack out of him, the only thing stopping him from crumbling. The only thing in this world that mattered to him right at this moment.

She looked up, eyes warm, soft and caring. "I wanted to say I'm sorry," she whispered. "I should never have asked you to go against your job, your principles."

He closed his eyes against a sudden sharp burn, put his head back, battling to keep it all inside. But she cupped the back of his head, made him look at her, and she leaned up on tiptoe and kissed him.

Through her summer dress he could feel her breasts, her nipples hardening, and he felt himself implode. He had to make love to her. Right now. In Epstein's hotel. Jenna's mouth opened warm, soft under his. Kissing her, Lex backed toward the check-in desk. "A room," he murmured against her lips. "We need a room."

They started up in the elevator, his tongue tangling with hers as he slipped his hand under her dress. He lifted her bare leg, smooth as silk, hooked it around him, finding her panties damp. His heart began to race, his breath coming short. Knowing the cameras, the eye-in-the-sky was watching, he thrust his fingers inside her, began to move them. Jenna sagged against him, sinking down onto his fingers, deepening his reach as she hooked her leg higher. He felt her undoing his fly, taking his erection into her hands.

She hurriedly guided him into herself, and Lex grabbed her buttocks as she curled her other leg around his hips and they crashed back against the mirror. With near-blind passionate hunger, a desperate need to find himself, to find her, he thrust up into her. She threw her head back, hair cascading down her back as she clung her arms around his neck.

This was one thing that felt true, real, right…and he pumped into her, fast, repeatedly, supporting her weight as she gasped, one hand sliding on the steamy mirror the other flying back to grip the railing as she came with a sharp cry, just as the bell clanged onto their floor.

Chapter 12

Stumbling backward into the room, kissing, they backed clumsily toward the bed, door slamming shut behind them. Lex dropped Jenna onto the covers, lifted her dress over her head and removed her panties. She moved her hands to his hips, slid his pants down his powerful thighs, exhilaration burning in her chest. "All of you," she whispered. "I want to see all of you."

It was turning to dusk outside, the vibrant flickering wattage of Vegas pulsing hotter as the sky over the desert dimmed to mute purples and browns. The light from the window was surreal, and it made him look like something from an erotic dream—Mediterranean skin olive and smooth, his muscles pumped with energy, literally vibrating for the same kind of release she'd had in the elevator. His hair hung in a loose lick over his forehead, and his features were predatory, etched with hunger for her, eyes fierce dark emeralds—something had shifted in him. Something had been set loose—primal and aggressive. And hot damn, she liked it.

Jenna grasped his wrists, yanked him down onto the bed and straddled him, hair falling wild over her shoulders. His eyes grew smoky, lids lowering as she sunk down onto his erection like a hot, wet glove, moving her hips until he groaned, grabbed her buttocks hard with powerful hands. He was still rock-hard from the elevator, and she was heating, tingling, for release all over again.

And with sudden shock, Jenna came, an explosion of muscular contractions that seized her body with glorious, gut-punching power. Lex couldn't hold back a second longer. He swung her roughly around onto all fours, took her from behind, squeezing her breasts, pulling her into his pelvis as he thrust and she arched her back, lustrous hair dark against creamy skin.

Lex's world shifted as he came with such fierce release that it shattered his body and mind, obliterating everything he'd just learned upstairs, and they fell back, breathless, sated. Lex held her, stroking her hair, his body still shimmering with latent energy, knowing, at the same time, that he'd never be the same. He'd found truth. In more ways than one. And not in the way he'd expected. Because the real truth lay right here in his arms, and so did his future—if he played it all right. And he realized, with irony, that while he'd come to Vegas seeking his past, instead he'd found the road that led ahead. Perhaps that's what he'd wanted all along.

Jenna rolled onto her side and traced her fingers over his abs, down the thick line of hair that ran to his groin, and she smiled wickedly as he began to swell again in front of her eyes.

"Careful," he whispered.

"Why?" she tickled the backs of her nails a little lower.

"Because I'm not done with you yet."

Jenna moved her hand to his groin, took hold of him, slid her knee up over his legs. Rolling closer, she moved her lips close to his, breasts pressing against his chest. "Did you mean it, Lex?" she murmured against his mouth.

"Mean what?"

She inhaled sharply as she felt him enter her.

"When…you said—" her voice came out thick, breathy as he moved, slow strokes that made her eyes roll back into her head "—that…you loved me? Was it true?"

He swung himself on top of her, deepened his thrust. She couldn't concentrate.

"Jenna—" his voice was husky "—you are the one thing in my life right now that is true."

"Boy, you're one sorry puppy, Lex Duncan, considering… *ah*—" He thrust hard and she arched. He came quickly. And they sank back, glowing with perspiration.

"Yes," he whispered up to the ceiling in the growing dark. "It is true."

He did love her.

He felt her hand slip into his, squeeze, and Lex's heart swelled to busting point.

"It's this," Lex said, tilting his chin toward the skyline. "This has got to be what people love about this place." They were sitting immersed in a hot tub full of bubbles, drinking from champagne flutes, looking out the floor-to-ceiling window at the Vegas night.

"Making love?" she said with a smile, hair piled loosely up on her head, tendrils wet, skin flushed.

He slanted his eyes to hers. "No, the fact that magic *can* happen," he whispered.

She studied him in silence. "What happened to you today, Lex?"

"What makes you think anything happened?

"You're…different. I don't know how to describe it. Intense. Edgy. Alive in a way that almost feels…dangerous."

His features turned serious. He trailed his fingers along her collarbone. "I found out who my father was today, Jenna," he said softly.

"What?"

He turned to look out over the view again, silent. "I was also informed that Sara Duncan was not my real mother."

She sat up. "Lex?"

He smiled ruefully. "You're so beautiful, Jenna." He glanced up into her eyes. "Do you think we could make it work? Do you think we could try?"

Emotion burned fast and sharp into her eyes. "Is…is this a proposal of some kind?" she whispered.

"Do you think you could love me, Jenna?"

She looked at him for several long moments, and his eyes grew worried.

"I think," she whispered, "that I fell in love with you the first time I saw you on—"

"Please, do not say on that god-awful auction stage."

"No, Lex, on that drought-brown football field. With your boys. I saw a leader, a man with an incredibly strong moral compass. And…" Emotion tightened her throat. "You made me think I…might want a family of my own one day. I'd never thought that before. You made me want more, Lex, something very different to what I have."

He glanced away sharply, features twisting, and Jenna saw tears glisten in his eyes…real damn tears. In her FBI agent. "God," he whispered, not daring to look at her. "You have no idea…absolutely no idea what that does to me."

"Tell me," she said softly, reaching out, cupping his jaw, turning his face back to hers. "Tell me about your mother, Lex. About your father."

He inhaled deeply. "Mercedes Epstein claims to be my mother, Jenna."

"What?"

"She said she paid Sara Duncan to register me in Reno and to raise me as her own son."

Her mouth fell open. "I…I don't understand. Does that mean Frank Epstein is—"

"My father? No. Mercedes apparently had an affair with a man named Tony Ciccone. You ever heard of him, Jenna?"

"Yes," she said very quietly. "He was the gangster who disappeared, the subject of one of the FBI's biggest manhunts at the time. He had a crazy temper, was a violent mob enforcer."

"And he was my father."

She looked at him, dumbstruck.

"Yeah," he said with a wry twist in his mouth. "Ironic, huh? The straight-shooting, button-up law enforcement officer has one of the most infamous mobsters in Nevada history as his dad. How's that supposed to make me feel, Jenna? What of that monster lurks in my DNA, under my skin, in the beat of my heart?"

"Lex, listen to me. That single-mindedness, that ferocity that was apparently Tony Ciccone, you might have it in you, but you chose to use it for good, for justice."

"It's weird, isn't it? They say that the profile of a cop is often closest to that of a criminal."

"But one is for good and the other bad."

He snorted. "If it were so simple."

"Hey," she said, leaning forward. "I know how blurred those lines get, remember? I was the one hiding stuff from homicide investigators. You showed me there *was* a line though and that I had to pick a side. I did, Lex. And you yourself, long ago, picked your side, too—the side of justice, when that Reno sheriff…what was his name?"

"Tom McCall, Washoe Country sheriff."

"Yes, when Tom pulled you back from trouble, he showed you where that line lay, Lex. He set you on track, and just think of all those kids that you've done the same for. You might have your father's genes in you, but maybe he never got the same chance that you did back in his own childhood." She gazed at him intently. "Maybe he didn't find a Tom McCall, but he found a Frank Epstein and mob family instead. What you do, Lex, is honorable. And you told me yourself that you do it because you love."

And God he loved *her* for reminding him of this, telling him what he so desperately needed to hear. For being here for him, nothing to hide between them any longer.

"Tell me, Lex. Everything."

She sat quietly and listened to the rest of his story, the whole story, including how he'd seen the man he believed had murdered Sara Duncan.

"How come you didn't go after him right away?"

"Because I need to do it right—I want a charge of murder, and I want it to stick. For that to happen, I still need evidence. All I have is a memory of a voice, and a conviction that Markowitz is the man I saw."

"What about Mercedes's story?"

"She could deny she said anything. Besides, she doesn't know who actually killed Sara, or so she says."

"What are you going to do?"

"First I see if Ciccone's remains really are down in that mine shaft. That's step one, hard evidence that can be used to have the Sara Duncan homicide case reopened. Then I hand this case over, because I am a victim and a witness. Next Ciccone's body goes for autopsy, and Mercedes is brought in for questioning based on what she told me. It'll have to be done soon if she's as ill as she claims to be."

"So Epstein doesn't know any of this?"

"Mercedes says she kept it from him."

Jenna snorted softly. "That's so ironic—Roman Markowitz, Tony Ciccone's old henchman, now working for Epstein as his security head…and neither Mercedes or Frank Epstein know."

"It looks that way."

"It's weird. Because I know a little about Roman Markowitz through the event planning business," said Jenna. "And from what I understand, Markowitz got his break in the security business at the old Frontline."

"Well, if he was working for Epstein back then, he'd have had to have been doing Ciccone's bidding on the sly, the bastard."

Jenna shook her head. "Mercedes is your mother… I still can't believe it. Do you think that's why she came to my auction, to see you?"

"So she says."

"And it's why she supports all those orphan charities?"

"Again, it's what she claims."

"I feel sorry for her, Lex, in a way."

"Why, she gave her kid away? Basically paid cash to get rid of me, because she didn't have the stomach for an abortion?"

"And she's been haunted by guilt ever since. I think deep down she's a good woman, Lex."

"You know something, Jenna—you're generous. With your heart. To a fault, even. You don't need money when you have real wealth like yours."

Her eyes filled with tears. "Lex, not one person in my life has ever said anything so beautiful, so meaningful to me. Thank you," she whispered.

He took her into his arms, all slippery soap bubbles and fragrance, and crushed his mouth to hers. "Jenna—" he said pulling back abruptly as it dawned on him. "How'd you know I'd be here, at the Desert Lion?"

"Rita told me. I went to find you, to…" Her eyes darkened.

"Geez, Lex, I almost forgot. I wanted to know if you'd heard about the Lucky Lady, Marion Robb. I read about her in the morning paper."

"What about her?"

"She was murdered. Last night. Her throat was slit."

He sat up abruptly. *"What?"*

"Yes, I thought—"

Urgency crackled through him. "I've got to get you out of this hotel, Jenna. Get dressed, at once. When we walk out that door, you act like nothing is wrong. Understand?"

"What are you saying, Lex?"

"Marion Robb's death cannot be coincidence. Someone must have been following us, learned I was looking for answers and was worried because Lucky Lady knew something. Something that would lead me back *here,* to Markowitz. Quick, move!"

"You…you think Markowitz knows you're onto him?" she said, stepping out of the tub, grabbing a towel.

"God alone knows." Lex pulled on his pants. "Marion didn't give me anything other than a hint at old mob connections, but I believe she had more to tell. She clammed up suddenly when I told her about that cartoon logo on the Cadillac—she *knew* something, Jenna, and it scared her. I was going to go back, build her trust, ease her into talking, over time."

Time that had just run out for her.

Lex grabbed his shirt. "*If* Markowitz is responsible for slitting her throat, he either believes I got something out of her, or she might have told him she'd stayed mum, and he killed her to keep it that way. Markowitz might still believe he is safe from me, as long as he doesn't make a stupid move. But I'm not taking chances, Jenna. I want you out of this hotel, *now.*"

He buttoned up his shirt as he called Perez. "I need you at the Desert Lion."

"I'm here, right outside. Followed Rothchild after telling her where you were." She yawned theatrically into the phone. "What's taking you two so long? What in the hell are you up to, Duncan?"

"I'll explain—"

"Heard that one before, partner. Not buying it again."

"Perez," he said urgently. "I'm into something. I want you to take Jenna home, far away from me. Close protection detail. Understand?"

"Duncan—"

"I believe I know who killed my mother. He's in this hotel, and he might get wind I'm onto him. That'll make him a very dangerous man, and I don't want Jenna anywhere near me if and when that happens. I think he's behind the death of Marion Robb, owner of the Lucky Lady psychic store on East—"

"Duncan, this is—"

"Just listen to me, Perez. Contact the LVMPD. Tell them the Lucky Lady homicide case is ours. Then get someone to look into a man named Roman Markowitz. He's security head at the Desert Lion. He apparently goes way back with Epstein, to the Tony Ciccone days. Maybe Markowitz whacked the psychic himself or had someone do it for him. Tell whoever takes the case to see if they can link Markowitz to that homicide. DNA, whatever. Anything."

"And where are you going?" Her tone had changed. She was sensing the seriousness in him.

"To find Ciccone's body."

Silence.

"You still there, Perez?"

"Are you okay, Duncan? You haven't lost it on me have you?"

"Jenna will fill you in." He hung up, felt for his weapon, chambered a round and held it ready, under his jacket, knowing the eye-in-the-sky would be on them the instant they exited the door. He took Jenna's arm, ushered her out the door and they started moving swiftly along soft carpet to the elevators.

Two suits appeared at the other end of the passage. Security. The men started to move toward them.

Lex had to force a smooth, casual pace. He pressed the elevator button, watching the men nearing in his peripheral vision. The elevator bell pinged, doors opening painfully slowly. He ushered Jenna in, jabbed the lobby button, pulse accelerating.

The elevator doors closed just as the security men passed by.

Two floors down, another security employee got into the car, but so did a middle-aged couple. Lex positioned Jenna behind the couple, using them as cover. Tense, they stood in silence as the car hummed slowly down. The doors opened. Lex put his arm around Jenna, sticking very close to the middle-aged couple, keeping them between the security employee and Jenna.

They exited the massive hotel doors and were hit by a wall of dark, damp heat. Perez was there, in her SUV, engine running. She leaned over and flung open the passenger door.

"Do you think any of this has anything to do with The Tears of the Quetzal, or Candace's death?" Jenna asked quietly as Lex held the door open for her.

"All I know is that ring led me down this road, Jenna." In more ways than one. Lex glanced at his partner, his eyes saying it all: *Be careful. Candace Rothchild's killer is still out there and someone still wants to hurt Jenna.*

"Lex—" Jenna's eyes were big, dark. A man could lose himself in those eyes "—be careful, okay? I…I have plans for us."

"Hey, I'm not going anywhere," he bent down to kiss her quickly. "I've got some plans of my own."

"Agent Duncan forgets—" Frank Epstein said quietly, observing Lex and Jenna exit his hotel "—that everyone watches everyone in Vegas, all the time. And," he added, "some men even watch their wives."

Roman Markowitz studied his boss in silence, his posture rigid.

Frank pinched the bridge of his nose, replaying in his mind what he'd witnessed on the monitor through the private feed into his own living room. None of what had transpired between Mercedes and Lex Duncan was news to him. Frank knew his wife was dying—he was in touch with Mercedes's doctor and paid him very well to keep him informed. He'd also known from day one that Tony Ciccone had been screwing his wife, that she'd tried to hide the pregnancy from him. He'd have whacked the little Italian bastard himself if Mercedes hadn't done it for him. And he loved her for it.

Besides, it had solved a very thorny little problem for him. Ciccone's mysterious vanishing act had kept the FBI off his back.

He'd always wanted Mercedes to have an illusion of freedom, but in effect, he controlled every aspect of her life. His sleight-of-hand, his trickery, had always been for her own good. He'd always protected her. Yet to the world she was independent, proud, regal—his Vegas queen. And he wanted her to die proud. On her terms. Under her own illusions. He loved her that much, that fiercely.

She'd become much more deeply religious and spiritual since she'd learned of her terminal illness. And in doing so, she'd become even more poignantly beautiful to him. So fragile in so many ways.

But now Lex Duncan knew her truth.

He knew Mercedes had shot and killed a man.

And the look Frank had glimpsed in the agent's eyes when Mercedes had confessed this—he'd seen that intent look before in another man. In the eyes of mob enforcer Tony Ciccone.

A bit of the father in the son, he thought to himself. You can't get away from that, Lexington.

A man like Lex Duncan, Frank could use on his side. On the wrong side… "He's dangerous now," he whispered.

Markowitz held his hand toward the monitor. "He still doesn't know who whacked his mother," he rasped. "You saw him on camera, and I saw him in that elevator. He doesn't know who I am. He has no idea."

Frank whipped to him, fury expressing violently through his blood. "It's not you I'm worried about, Roman," he said calmly. He looked at his nails, trying to defuse the pressure fizzing inside him. "You might have been working for Ciccone as my spy into his inner machinations at a time I really needed to know the extent of his operations, and what he might use against me. But—" he looked up "—you never should have killed that woman when he chose to send you to kidnap the boy."

"The bitch shot me."

"And your temper remains too short for your own good. No, Roman, it's not you I'm concerned about, it's my wife. It's *me*— I don't want this ancient Ciccone crap coming back to sit on me now. And I simply cannot allow my wife to suffer at the hands of the FBI, be taken in, interrogated, possibly charged for murder in her last days."

She needed to go in peace. And Frank was prepared to kill to ensure this.

Markowitz cleared his throat. "You want me to take him out, sir?"

"It's imperative." He breathed his words out softly, like he so often did when he was about to blow. "My regret is that we did not have them put into one of our rooms wired with camera and sound. We have no idea what Duncan told the Rothchild woman while he was screwing her."

He inhaled deeply, trying to ease the hammering in his skull, his skin heating at the thought of them fornicating in his own elevator, under sight of his cameras. And Duncan doing it with a daughter of Harold Rothchild of all women. It was the ultimate slap in his face, in the face of his wife and his entire establishment. If he wasn't going to have the man killed, Frank would have his badge. He'd release the sexual footage to the mainstream media—a federal agent screwing the sister of a homicide victim, a case on which he was the lead investigator. Duncan had to know he was being watched. The bastard. It was like he no longer cared…which worried Frank. A little.

"So we do her, too," said Markowitz in his scratchy voice. "Just in case."

Frank tilted his chin slightly toward the monitor. "That's an FBI vehicle he's putting her into."

"I can have someone on that SUV in seconds. Just say it, boss, and I give the order."

"Do it."

Markowitz reached for a special cell, one he used only for very discreet jobs. Like the contract killing of a casino heiress and her FBI bodyguard. Like the elimination of a psychic with too much knowledge.

"It's me," he rasped into the phone. "This one must look like an accident. Affirmative—all occupants of the vehicle. Same payment structure."

He looked up, flipping his phone shut. "Done."

"Good. Now come with me. We're taking a little drive into the Mojave to remove Ciccone's remains. This time, the ghost of Ciccone will vanish for good."

"What about Duncan?"

"Trust me, he'll go straight out there to look for Ciccone's body. We'll be there waiting for him, take care of him ourselves."

"I can send someone—"

"No. We do it. You and me. No more loose ends."

Roman eyed his boss. Warily. A cold fist of tension curling in his abdomen.

* * *

Lex closed the door, stood back, banged the roof of the vehicle. "Go!"

The SUV moved on. Lex exhaled, dragging his hand over his hair as he watched the vehicle disappearing into the soaking hot, airless night, sweat already forming on his skin.

Geez, was he being overly paranoid? But he couldn't bear the idea off losing her. Not now.

Not ever.

Jenna had just given him a glimpse into a future, shown him what he really wanted, what they could have together. But that meant he now had everything to lose.

He told himself she'd be safe with Perez until he got back. Perez was a top agent, experienced. Sharp. He breathed out a hot sigh, allowing tension to ease just a little as he made for his own vehicle.

When Lex left the rambling city perimeter, taking the road that would lead to the old ghost town, the desert night grew thick and dark. Stars spattered the black dome of sky. And tension torqued inside him. He felt under the dash for his flashlight and an extra clip for his weapon.

Chapter 13

Rita Perez drew her SUV up to the security booth at the Roth-child mansion. She depressed the brakes, scrolling her window down as she reached for her badge.

But before either Jenna or Rita could even register what was happening, a man dressed completely in black with a balaclava pulled over his head stepped in front of Rita's passenger window. He aimed a gun fitted with a suppressor into the car. Behind him, lying on the driveway, dark blood glistening in her car headlights, Jenna saw the limp body of her dad's security guard.

She screamed.

As she did, Rita reached for her weapon, ducking and pushing Jenna below the dash in the same motion. But as Rita moved, the man fired.

The shot was quiet, like in an assassin movie.

Jenna felt Rita's body jerk hard, and then shudder. The agent slumped limply on top of her. Hot blood came gushing from a wound on her head. Terror dumped through Jenna's nerves. She pushed Rita's body off her and stared in sheer horror at the ragged wound in the agent's skull, the way her mouth hung slack and open. The man with the black balaclava was moving quickly round to Jenna's door. He yanked it open, his gun now aimed at her. "You! Get in the back!" he hissed, grabbing her upper arm.

A small squeak came from somewhere low in Jenna's throat as she tried to scream and jerk free of his grasp. But the man raised his pistol and struck a glancing blow off her temple.

Her world went black.

When she came round, she felt nauseous. It took a few sickening, dizzying moments to realize she was bound tightly with rope and lying in the back of Rita's SUV. Rita's body lay limp and bloody beside her.

And the car was moving, somewhere dark. In the desert, no lights anywhere around them.

Headlights cut through blackness along a faraway ridge. The beams were then swallowed as the vehicle emitting them dipped into a canyon. There was only one road up ahead as far as Lex knew, and it led to the ghost town.

A sense of foreboding rustled through him.

Could be teens, out for a party, he thought. Or something more sinister.

He pulled abruptly over to the side of the road and examined his map with his flashlight. There was a much older disused track that led around the back of the abandoned town. It was several miles longer, but if he used that track, he could approach the town from the rear unanticipated. He could park his SUV below a ridge to the west, cut his lights, climb up and over the ridge, advancing in silence. If there was anyone in that old ghost town, he'd have the advantage of being able to see who they were, where they were and what they were up to.

He quickly removed his white shirt, reached back into the passenger seat and extracted a dark long-sleeved T-shirt from his gym bag. He pulled it over his head, checked his weapon and restarted the ignition.

Lex crept up the back of the ridge. The night was cloaked thick with heat, dead silent. The uncanny quietness set him on edge, heightened his senses. He could smell sand, stone, feel residual heat radiating up from sand that had blistered under the desert sun. He crested the ridge.

Below him silver moonlight glowed eerily over ruined buildings that squatted in a valley of dry scrub. A knotted ball of tumbleweed lodged at the facade of a crumbling structure, shades of gray and black playing tricks with his eyes. Lex could make out the shape of an old oil drum, a rusted old truck—remains of a life, an industry. Long gone. A mine headframe loomed above the abandoned structures, throwing long distorted shadows over the landscape.

There's a main headframe, easy to spot. Next to it is an old metal-sided building. If you go about two hundred yards east of that, you'll find another shaft opening covered with metal grate. He's down there...

Lex shifted his gaze eastward, and suddenly he saw it—an SUV parked at the far end of the buildings, moonlight glinting off chrome.

Sliding his pistol from its holster, he scrambled sideways down the steep drop, dislodging a shower of small pebbles that went skittering down the bank ahead of him, sound disproportionately loud. Lex stilled at the bottom, pulse quickening. He waited. Silence descended back on the ghost town, and he crept stealthily toward the hulking buildings.

The sudden creak and groan of metal grating cut through the stillness, and again Lex froze. He edged further along the front of the metal-sided building, gun held down and in front of his body, making his way two hundred yards east of the rusting headframe as per Mercedes's directions. He stopped. He could hear voices now. Males. Two.

He crept closer, ducked down behind a rusted drum, listened.

And he heard the sound that had haunted his boyhood dreams—the distinct sandpapery voice of Roman Markowitz. Lex peered cautiously around the wall. And he saw Frank Epstein in the pale moonlight.

They'd come ahead of him.

But how had they known? This was supposed to be Mercedes's dark secret from her husband. The thought struck him suddenly…could Epstein have had a camera in his own penthouse, been watching her whole confession? Was Mercedes in trouble now—or worse? Lex's heart began to slam as an even more chilling thought scrambled goose bumps over his skin—what if Epstein had a camera planted in his and Jenna's hotel room? If so, Epstein would know that Jenna knew everything.

Had Lex put *her* life in danger?

His head began to swim. *Focus.* Jenna was with Perez. If he made a rash move now, he could end up dead. And dead wasn't going to help Jenna. He couldn't phone her now, either. The men would hear. Nor could he call for back-up.

Lex inched farther forward, lowering himself behind the cover of a rusting boxcar. From there he watched Markowitz descend into the mine shaft using rungs grafted against the wall.

Markowitz's granular voice carried eerily up the mine shaft, which seemed to function as a large bullhorn. "He's down here, all right, boss, I see bones." Markowitz swore. "He's like a freaking mummy. D'you want to throw that bag, and I'll package him, bring him up?"

Lex peered farther around the boxcar, saw the dark shape of

Frank Epstein directing a powerful flashlight down the shaft. The heavy grate that had covered it lay to one side. Pulling back that grate must have been what caused the sound Lex had heard earlier.

"You sure it's him?" Epstein called down the shaft.

"Yeah, yeah the ring…it's Ciccone's ring, the one with the gold seal." He swore. "Geez, his finger bones just fell off when I touched him."

"I want to see for myself. Wait there—I'm coming down."

Another wave of goose bumps chased over Lex's skin as he saw Epstein draw a handgun from a holster at his ankle, check it, chamber a round and replace his weapon. Damn, the bastard was going to kill Markowitz? When? Once they got the bones bagged and back up into the SUV?

Lex's brain raced.

He needed the evidence to remain where it was. And he couldn't call for backup now. They'd hear. He needed to find a way to incapacitate these two, maybe trap them down in the shaft with the remains of Ciccone. Hold them until help arrived.

Epstein began to lower himself carefully into the shaft, the beam of his flashlight catching dust that floated up from the disturbed tomb below.

"Careful, Mr. Epstein. It's steep and not very secure. Are you sure?"

"Of course I'm sure."

"What about Duncan—what if he arrives while we're down here?"

"We'd already have seen him coming miles away on that road. We can set an ambush for him once we've got Ciccone bagged."

Lex waited for Epstein's head to sink below ground level. The minute he was down there, Lex would make for the heavy grate, seal them in from the top.

But just before Epstein was swallowed by the earth, Lex's phone buzzed loudly in his pocket. He swore to himself, jerked back, fumbled quickly in his pocket. He was about to click it off but saw the number in the green glow. Lex put the phone to his ear. "Yes," he whispered, quiet as he could.

"Special Agent Duncan, it's Agent Savalas. We've got a situation—"

Lex tensed.

"There's a security guard down at the Rothchild mansion, and security footage shows a man in a black balaclava firing a weapon into Agent Perez's vehicle. He then got into the vehicle and left the scene."

His heart twisted violently. "Jenna? Perez?"

"He's got them."

"Are they injured?" Lex whispered, hoarse. In the back of his mind he heard the men in the mineshaft go quiet—God, they'd heard him!

"We don't know. And we have no fix on the vehicle—"

"Perez's vehicle is fitted with GPS. Track it. Call me as soon as you have a location. I'm coming in."

He killed the call.

Silence rung loud in his ears. Just the thud of his heart.

Lex swore to himself, panic whispering seductively at the edges of his consciousness. Was it the same man who'd fired at her during the car chase?

Footfalls crunched in dirt, advancing. *The two men were coming for him.* They must have scrambled back out of the shaft when they'd heard him, and he'd been distracted.

Lex heard the rack of a rifle.

Fire boiled into his blood. He refused to lose. If he did, Jenna would die.

A gunshot pinged suddenly off the side of the boxcar, near his head.

Lex ducked down. They definitely knew he was here. Alone

in the desert. Two against one. Lex scurried along the base of
the boxcar, dashed in a crouch across a gap and tucked in
behind a shed, staying low and quiet. Those two men were a
good deal older than him. And he was now fired with raw determination like nothing he'd known, a passion that was consuming him whole. All those men were to Lex now was an
obstacle in his way to saving Jenna.

She was his priority.

Not Epstein.

Not the man who'd killed his mother—not any longer.

Lex had reached a tipping point, and he'd gone over the
edge, seen what lay on the other side. A future. With a woman
who'd bewitched him within three minutes flat—the duration
of the song that had played on the dance floor only four nights
ago, before the big clock in the Ruby Room had struck twelve.
Lex had known it back then, deep down, that he was toast.

Blame it on The Tears of the Quetzal curse. Blame it on Vegas
fate, chance, luck, magic. Whatever it was, he wasn't going to
let Jenna go now. He was going to be her protector 24/7. For the
rest of his life. And these bastards were simply in his way.

Another shot pinged off the boxcar where Lex had been just
seconds ago. It gave the gunman's position away. Lex peered
round the shed, squeezed off two shots. Immediately gunfire
returned. Lex ducked, aimed again, this time the shooter went
down with a grunt and thud in the dirt. It was Markowitz.

Lex now aimed for Epstein, who was running for his vehicle.
He fired into dirt at this feet. Dust kicked up in a small explosion. Epstein kept running. Lex stepped out from his cover,
weapon aimed at Epstein. "Halt! FBI!"

But Epstein kept moving. Lex squeezed off another round,
aiming for the sand at his feet.

Panting, Epstein stopped. He raised both hands, turned
slowly round. "Don't. Shoot."

Lex didn't waste time even acknowledging the bastard. His weapon trained on Epstein, he moved quickly toward the bag and length of rope they'd been going to use to raise Ciccone up from the shaft. He snagged the rope, approached Epstein, grabbed the old man, and shoved him brusquely onto his stomach in the sand.

"Wait…think this through, Duncan. I've got enough cash to—"

"You bastard," Lex snapped as he wrenched the grizzled old lion king's hands behind his back with the rope and hauled him to his feet. "When are you going to learn you can't buy everything, Epstein?" He shoved the stumbling, heavily-breathing man towards the SUV as he spoke.

"I can give you what you want—"

"I already got what I want. I'm going to see your entire empire go down into the dirt. Where are the keys?"

"I swear, you're going to regret this, Duncan. I have connections in places that—"

"Get in!" Lex barked as he yanked open the back hatch. "On your stomach."

"Duncan—"

He pressed the muzzle of his gun into the old mobster's back. "Do it! Now!"

Once the old man was humiliatingly bundled into his own trunk, Lex hogtied him, looping the rope so that Epstein's feet were bound to his hands. This desert king wasn't going anywhere but down.

Lex climbed into the driver's seat, dialing dispatch as he started the ignition. "Connect me with someone who can give me a fix on the GPS in Agent Perez's vehicle!" he barked. "And I need backup as soon as we get a reading on where she is." He hit the gas as he spoke, giving dispatch a rundown of the situation. And with Epstein swearing in the back, he raced back toward the city of Las Vegas, toward the gold halo of light in the desert, dust boiling in a dark cone behind him. Lex had no idea which direction to go, but this was a start until he had a fix on Perez's location. There was no way he could just sit and do nothing while he waited.

He called both Jenna's and Perez's phones as he drove. Both kept flipping to voice mail. Tension torqued like a vise in him.

His phone buzzed. Lex snapped it to his ear. "Yes!"

"We have a location. Perez's vehicle is stationary at a place called Bucktooth Ranch, an old property that was sold and slated for demolition two years ago, but redevelopment permits have been on hold because of legal issues—"

"I know it!" Lex hit the brakes, wheeling sharply as he pulled a 180 degree turn off-road. The car fishtailed into sand, dust billowing in a cloud around him as he bounced wildly over rugged terrain, dry scrub scraping the undercarriage of the SUV as he aimed for an intersecting road about a mile ahead. "I'm not far out. I can be there in a few minutes," he yelled into his phone. "Get that tactical team out there stat!"

The SUV tires bit suddenly into harder packed dirt as his vehicle hit the intersecting road. He punched down on the gas, increasing speed. "I'm about eight miles out now. Can you give me the ranch specs? How many buildings?"

"A bunch of old cabins…seven to the left of a main building, which is derelict."

"Approach road?"

"One road in, dirt. There's also an old horse trail that hooks around to the west."

"Wide enough for an SUV?"

"Affirmative."

"I'm going in that way."

Lex cut his lights and engine.

In the distance a yellow glow spilled from a window in one

of the old log cabins. The dark shape of Perez's SUV was tucked in alongside the west wall of the cabin, facing outward, as if ready for a quick getaway.

Leaving Epstein hog-tied in the vehicle, Lex ran in a crouch through a stand of dry scrub. He came up under the window, peered carefully up through broken, dusty glass. A flickering lantern stood on an old wood table, cell phone lying next to it. He shifted his gaze to the left, and his heart stalled.

Jenna! Arms above her head, hands tied from the rafters. Her face sheet-white, streaked with dirt, tears, mascara, hair a wild tangle. A man in a black balaclava held a knife to the exposed column of her neck. He was trailing the hooked tip down to the hollow at the base of her throat.

Although the man's face was masked, he was familiar in height and build to Thomas Smythe, the man who'd threatened the life of exotic dancer Vera Mancuso.

He peered up a little higher, caught sight of Perez's body lying in a small heap in the darkened corner of the cabin. Lex struggled to draw in a breath, to hold his position. It was not known if Smythe was the same guy who'd murdered Candace, but Lex had seen enough during the standoff over Mancuso's life to know that if this was Smythe, he was no rational man. Smythe had wanted that ring. And he'd probably do anything first and foremost for The Quetzal. Lex ducked down, checked his watch, mentally calculating how long it would take for backup to reach this remote ranch.

Too long.

Especially if Perez was still hanging onto life, needing medical attention. Lex *had* to move. But if he did act now, without backup, he could cost Jenna's life. He peered up again.

The man tilted Jenna's chin up with the hooked blade of his knife. Fresh tears shimmered down her face. Lex saw blood on her dress. Was she injured? Was it Perez's blood?

The man began to trail the blade back down the column of her throat, moving his body closer to hers. Jenna tried to shrink away from him, arms straining visibly above her head. But the man hooked the knife tip into the top of her dress and jerked it down hard. The fabric split in a ragged gash, flaying open at her sides to reveal bare breasts and her skimpy scrap of a silky G-string. The man touched her nipple with his knife.

Blinding rage erupted in Lex.

He launched up, shouldered through the door. It smashed back with an explosive crash as he barreled into the room, his weapon aimed at the man. "Get back from her, now, you bastard, or you're dead," he growled, shaking inside, his arms steady as granite.

"Lex! Oh, God…" Tears poured down Jenna's face. She began shaking. Perez still lay lifeless in the far corner, blood congealing dark under her head, glistening in the lamplight.

The man swiftly pressed his blade to Jenna's neck. "Put the gun down," he ordered, a faint hint of Spanish accent coming out under stress. "Or I *will* cut her throat before you can squeeze off a shot."

Lex swallowed, the shaking inside turning his gut to jelly, but he remained calm on the outside—as controlled as he could possibly be. He stared into the man's eyes, dark-brown like Smythe's. "I brought the ring," he said quietly. "I have The Tears of the Quetzal. I think you want that diamond more than you want her."

Agitation rippled visibly through the man. He pressed the knife tighter against Jenna's throat, sweat glistening around his eyes. With his free hand he slid a handgun out from the back of his jeans and aimed it at Lex. "Put the ring and gun on the table."

"Easy, buddy. Release her first, and then you get the ring."

His eyes narrowed in his balaclava slit. "How'd you find me?

How'd you know to bring The Tears of the Quetzal? I didn't give you directions yet."

"I tracked Agent Perez's vehicle," Lex said coolly, forcing himself not to look at his partner lying in an unconscious heap in the corner. He needed to get her to a hospital. The seconds were ticking down, time running out. Yet he had to stretch time out perhaps until backup arrived, in order to save Jenna. Tension cinched like a vise inside Lex. "Now, why don't you step back, put your weapons down, and like I said, I will give you the ring."

"No, *you* put your gun down, and place the ring on the table."

Lex could hear the nerves increasing in the man's voice. Warning bells began to clang.

"That's not how it's going to work," said Lex. "And don't think of pulling that trigger, because you'll be a dead man before I even hit the ground."

The man pressed the blade of his knife tighter against Jenna's throat. She whimpered, shivering, half-naked, tears streaming all the way down her breasts now. Lex trembled with bottled rage inside.

"If you hurt her—" Lex said, voice ice cool, his mind racing and thinking of what Jenna told him about the death threats her father had hidden "—then I will kill you, and you will get nothing. No ring. No revenge for the old deed you mentioned in those notes to Harold Rothchild."

The man wavered.

Good, *this* was his guy, Smythe, and Lex had made a connection. "That's why you want the ring, isn't it? To fix some past wrong. The ring that is more important to you than the 'Rothchild trash,' am I right? You need that ring first. Without the ring, you have nothing."

The man's dark-brown eyes flickered. "Just…just put it on the table." The Spanish accent that had crept into his voice as tension and fear got to him was thickening. His hands were beginning to shake. The warning bells in the back of Lex's mind clanged louder.

"Something happened back in South America didn't it…an old deed that needs to be avenged?"

"The Rothchilds must pay!"

"Harold Rothchild? Or someone older perhaps? Like his father, Joseph Rothchild, maybe?"

Agitation suddenly grew very marked in the man. Sweat began to pool around his eyes. Big damp patches were forming under the arms of his black shirt. "Just put the damn ring on the table!"

"And if I do, what guarantee do I have that you won't do something stupid, like try to kill us both once you have The Tears of the Quetzal?" Lex kept repeating the name of the cursed stone. It clearly had an effect on Jenna's assailant.

The man's eyes darted to his right, and flicked back to the door. Lex followed his gaze, saw the trip wire. And another one. His heart began to slam. *Smythe had rigged the whole cabin.* This place was set to blow the minute he left here.

"Did you rig this place? Is that your plan?"

The man's eyes shot to the cell phone that lay on the table. So, thought Lex, that's probably how he was going to detonate his explosives once he'd left. Using the cell phone.

"Okay," Lex said slowly. "I'm going to put the ring down on the table now."

"Gun first."

"No. I keep my gun." Lex moved his hand to his pocket, and the guy got instantly jumpy, shoving his knife tight against Jenna's throat.

"Easy, buddy, I'm just reaching for the ring, okay?" Lex extracted his wallet from his pocket, leaned forward, placed it on the table. "It's in there."

"Take it out."

"No. You take it out."

The man's eyes were fixated on the wallet. His whole body began to shake with desperation to snatch the ring he believed was in the wallet. They were locked in a standoff now.

Then Lex heard it, the distant sound of approaching vehicles.

The man picked up the sound, too. Panic flared in his dark eyes behind the mask. And Lex saw him struggling mentally, pulled by the powerful lure of the ring. Abruptly the man swung his gun, fired at the lantern. The glass exploded, lantern flying back and clattering to the floor. The room went dark, small flames licking through spilled lantern fuel.

Lex saw the man lunge for the wallet and cell phone, but he couldn't risk shooting in the flickering shadows from this angle. Instead, he moved on instinct to block Jenna's body should the man fire.

Headlights suddenly illuminated the desert outside as FBI vehicles crested the distant ridge, and Lex saw the shadow of the assailant as he fled out the door. Flames were licking into dry wood, smoke filling the cabin. Lex quickly groped on the floor for the blade the man had dropped in his desperation to grab the ring, and he cut Jenna free. She collapsed into his arms. "Oh, thank God," she whispered, her face wet against his neck, her body soft and beautiful in his arms. "Jenna, you okay? Are you hurt anywhere?"

"I'm fine, but Perez—"

Lex moved quickly over to his partner's limp form, felt her neck. "She has a pulse! Get out there, Jenna! Tell them we need an ambulance. Bomb squad. And get as far away from this building as you can!"

Holding her ripped dress together, Jenna ran outside to warn the FBI team as Lex gathered Perez in his arms, and staggered out of the smoke-filled burning cabin.

It exploded behind him in a whoosh of orange, sparks brilliant in the desert sky. Fire began to crackle fiercely, and black smoke billowed up to blot the stars.

Lex stood in the dark desert with his arm around Jenna as they watched firefighters extinguish what was left of the blazing cabins. Jenna was wearing a tracksuit provided to her by a female member of the tactical response team, and had a blanket draped over her shoulders. Paramedics had checked her out, and crime scene techs had taken evidence from beneath her nails—she'd managed to gouge her assailant's neck as he'd fought to truss her up to the rafters.

Her attacker had, however, managed to slip like a ghost into the Nevada night. He was in for a small surprise when he learned there was no diamond in Lex's wallet.

Meanwhile, Epstein had been taken into custody, and Perez had been rushed to hospital after being stabilized on the scene.

"You think Rita is going to be okay?" Jenna said.

"I believe it with all my heart," said Lex. "The paramedics said she was lucky. The bullet just grazed her skull. She lost a lot of blood and received a bad concussion, but she was already starting to regain consciousness when the ambulance left." Too bad Perez hadn't managed to get a glimpse of her assailant, thought Lex. They had no definite proof it was Smythe.

Jenna slipped her arms around his waist, holding him so tight, like she never wanted to let him go. And Lex knew immediately what he must do—take her away. Get off the case. Get the hell out of Vegas until that maniac was caught.

Until his woman was safe.

He didn't care if it cost his job, his career, anything else, as long as he kept her.

Forever.

He was not going to allow Jenna out of his sight for a minute. His heart brimming with emotion—and purpose—Lex turned to face her. Cupping the back of her neck, he threaded his fingers up into her thick lustrous tangle of hair and tilted her jaw up with his thumb. "Jenna, I may not have had The Tears of the Quetzal on me, but I *do* have a diamond," he whispered.

"What…do you mean?"

"I can see it, in my mind. So real. Small—tiny in fact— nothing like The Tears of Quetzal. But it's pure, Jenna. A tiny faultless blue-white. As clean and real and enduring as I want things to be for us. And when I do find that little stone, I…" His voice caught. "I want you to wear it."

She stared up at him, eyes beginning to mist in the darkness.

"Will you, Jenna? Just try it on for size while you see if you want to be my wife?"

He felt a small tremor shudder through her body. Tears began streaming down her face again. "Lex—"

Worry wedged into his heart.

"Only while we try, Jenna. Promise me—"

"Lex," she whispered. "You're pumped on adrenaline, anger…maybe…maybe this should wait until—"

"I don't need to wait."

"It's only been four days, how…how can you *possibly* be sure?"

"I'm as sure, Jenna, as I was when that clock struck midnight in the great Ruby Room, that I wanted nothing else but my casino princess. But if you're not ready—" he hesitated, unsure of what the hell he'd do if she said no.

"Oh, God, no I *am* ready, Lex. I've been waiting for you all my life. I…I just didn't know it. I just couldn't believe that… you…that you would want me."

"Is that a yes?"

She leaned up on tiptoe, met his lips with hers. "That, Agent Duncan, would be a yes."

He kissed her, hard and fast and desperate in the thick desert night, and Jenna thought her heart would burst with sheer love. He'd freed her, come riding into her rarefied life like a knight in shining armor, and he'd shown her how to be real.

How to be true to the self she'd so long ago buried inside.

He'd given her herself.

Himself.

And the promise that came with a small true blue diamond— a future, together.

"Do you think it's true, Lex?" she whispered, lips burning from the raw possessive passion in his kiss.

"What?"

"The legend…the curse of The Tears of the Quetzal."

Lex laughed, feeling a strange tingling chill even as he did, recalling the words of the skydiver. "It's Vegas," he said softly. "Anything can happen here."

Even magic.

And he kissed her again under the desert stars, the quietly strobing lights of police vehicles nearby, the glow of a burning building.

And he'd never felt more centered. More whole. More at home, than with this woman in his arms. He'd found family. His own.

Epilogue

With Lex and Jenna off celebrating their engagement on a small and isolated Caribbean island with no electricity, no glitz, no glam—simple and real like they'd said they wanted it, Rita Perez had been asked to temporarily take over as lead agent on the Candace Rothchild homicide case.

Harold Rothchild's lawyers had cut a deal with the feds, handing over the notes he'd kept hidden from police, along with an earth-shattering old video of Frank Epstein brokering a mob deal back in the 1980s—evidence that would ultimately help the FBI dismantle the entire Epstein empire.

In turn, Rothchild's lawyers were seeking immunity for their client on other possible charges. It looked like Rothchild would walk free.

People with money got away with murder, thought Rita as she hung up her dishcloth, and put the last of her dinner dishes away. It also turned out that Rothchild's little trophy wife,

Rebecca Lynn, while acting suspiciously, had just been gunning for Jenna, insanely jealous of Harold's affection for his youngest daughter.

Mercedes Epstein, on the other hand, was in the hospital, the prognosis not good. But she had confessed to the murder of Tony Ciccone. And Frank Epstein, in trying to save his own neck, had given up everything he had on the dead Roman Markowitz. The 30-year-old cold case—Sara Duncan's homicide—was thus finally solved.

Epstein had also offered up the names of two contract killers who'd handled several jobs for Markowitz—including the murder of Marion Robb, aka Lucky Lady.

Rita flipped off the kitchen light, her head beginning to hurt again. Dinner with her niece Marisa and her man Patrick Moore had been wonderful, and Rita was real happy for Marisa, but she was worn out and needed sleep.

But before going to bed, she unlocked her gun safe and removed a small box. She just needed to see the contents just one more time.

Pulse quickening, Rita opened the box…and an ice-cold nausea swept into her chest.

The diamond was gone!

Rita stared at the empty box, her heart jackhammering, sweat forming over her body. She should never have brought The Tears of the Quetzal home. She couldn't even articulate why she'd done it, but she had.

She'd gone into that evidence room compelled by some strange force to take a look at the mysterious stone. And when she'd lifted the diamond out of the box and held it to the light, luminous shafts had darted out, picking up a rainbow of colors from green to gold to champagne. It had clean stolen her breath.

Along with her mind.

Overcome by a strangely powerful impulse, Rita had

slipped The Tears of the Quetzal into her pocket, locked the door and gone home.

And now The Tears of the Quetzal was missing...

* * * * *

Celebrate Harlequin's 60th anniversary with
Harlequin® Superromance®
and the DIAMOND LEGACY miniseries!

Follow the stories of four cousins as they come to terms with
the complications of love and what it means to be a family.
Discover with them the sixty-year-old secret that rocks not
one but two families in...
A DAUGHTER'S TRUST by Tara Taylor Quinn.

Available in September 2009 from
Harlequin® Superromance®

RICK'S APPOINTMENT with his attorney early Wednesday morning went only moderately better than his meeting with social services the day before. The prognosis wasn't great—but at least his attorney was going to file a motion for DNA testing. Just so Rick could petition to see the child…his sister's baby. The sister he didn't know he had until it was too late.

The rest of what his attorney said had been downhill from there.

Cell phone in hand before he'd even reached his Nitro, Rick punched in the speed dial number he'd programmed the day before.

Maybe foster parent Sue Bookman hadn't received his message. Or had lost his number. Maybe she didn't want to talk to him. At this point he didn't much care what she wanted.

"Hello?" She answered before the first ring was complete. And sounded breathless.

Young and breathless.

"Ms. Bookman?"

"Yes. This is Rick Kraynick, right?"

"Yes, ma'am."

"I recognized your number on caller ID," she said, her voice uneven, as though she was still engaged in whatever physical activity had her so breathless to begin with. "I'm sorry I didn't get back to you. I've been a little…distracted."

The words came in more disjointed spurts. Was she jogging?

"No problem," he said, when, in fact, he'd spent the better part of the night before watching his phone. And fretting. "Did I get you at a bad time?"

"No worse than usual," she said, adding, "Better than some. So, how can I help?"

God, if only this could be so easy. He'd ask. She'd help. And life could go well. At least for one little person in his family.

It would be a first.

"Mr. Kraynick?"

"Yes. Sorry. I was…are you sure there isn't a better time to call?"

"I'm bouncing a baby, Mr. Kraynick. It's what I do."

"Is it Carrie?" he asked quickly, his pulse racing.

"How do you know Carrie?" She sounded defensive, which wouldn't do him any good.

"I'm her uncle," he explained, "her mother's—Christy's— older brother, and I know you have her."

"I can neither confirm nor deny your allegations, Mr. Kraynick. Please call social services." She rattled off the number.

"Wait!" he said, unable to hide his urgency. "Please," he said more calmly. "Just hear me out."

"How did you find me?"

"A friend of Christy's."

"I'm sorry I can't help you, Mr. Kraynick," she said softly. "This conversation is over."

"I grew up in foster care," he said, as though that gave him some special privilege. Some insider's edge.

"Then you know you shouldn't be calling me at all."

"Yes… But Carrie is my niece," he said. "I need to see her. To know that she's okay."

"You'll have to go through social services to arrange that."

"I'm sure you know it's not as easy as it sounds. I'm a single man with no real ties and I've no intention of petitioning for custody. They aren't real eager to give me the time of day. I never even knew Carrie's mother. For all intents and purposes, our mother didn't raise either one of us. All I have going for me is half a set of genes. My lawyer's on it, but it could be weeks—months—before this is sorted out. Carrie could be adopted by then. Which would be fine, great for her, but then I'd have lost my chance. I don't want to take her. I won't hurt her. I just have to see her."

"I'm sorry, Mr. Kraynick, but…"

* * * * *

Find out if Rick Kraynick
will ever have a chance to meet his niece.
Look for A DAUGHTER'S TRUST by Tara Taylor Quinn,
available in September 2009.

**We'll be spotlighting a different series
every month throughout 2009
to celebrate our 60th anniversary.**

**Look for Harlequin® Superromance®
in September!**

*Celebrate with
The Diamond Legacy
miniseries!*

Follow the stories of four cousins as they come to terms
with the complications of love and what it means to
be a family. Discover with them the sixty-year-old secret
that rocks not one but two families.

A DAUGHTER'S TRUST by *Tara Taylor Quinn*
September

FOR THE LOVE OF FAMILY by *Kathleen O'Brien*
October

LIKE FATHER, LIKE SON by *Karina Bliss*
November

A MOTHER'S SECRET by *Janice Kay Johnson*
December

Available wherever books are sold.

REQUEST YOUR FREE BOOKS!

2 FREE NOVELS PLUS 2 FREE GIFTS!

Sparked by Danger, Fueled by Passion!

YES! Please send me 2 FREE Silhouette® Romantic Suspense novels and my 2 FREE gifts (gifts are worth about $10). After receiving them, if I don't wish to receive any more books, I can return the shipping statement marked "cancel." If I don't cancel, I will receive 4 brand-new novels every month and be billed just $4.24 per book in the U.S. or $4.99 per book in Canada. That's a savings of at least 15% off the cover price! It's quite a bargain! Shipping and handling is just 50¢ per book*. I understand that accepting the 2 free books and gifts places me under no obligation to buy anything. I can always return a shipment and cancel at any time. Even if I never buy another book from Silhouette, the two free books and gifts are mine to keep forever.

240 SDN EYL4 340 SDN EYMG

Name	(PLEASE PRINT)	
Address		Apt. #
City	State/Prov.	Zip/Postal Code

Signature (if under 18, a parent or guardian must sign)

Mail to the Silhouette Reader Service:
IN U.S.A.: P.O. Box 1867, Buffalo, NY 14240-1867
IN CANADA: P.O. Box 609, Fort Erie, Ontario L2A 5X3

Not valid to current subscribers of Silhouette Romantic Suspense books.

Want to try two free books from another line?
Call 1-800-873-8635 or visit www.morefreebooks.com.

* Terms and prices subject to change without notice. Prices do not include applicable taxes. Sales tax applicable in N.Y. Canadian residents will be charged applicable provincial taxes and GST. Offer not valid in Quebec. This offer is limited to one order per household. All orders subject to approval. Credit or debit balances in a customer's account(s) may be offset by any other outstanding balance owed by or to the customer. Please allow 4 to 6 weeks for delivery. Offer available while quantities last.

Your Privacy: Silhouette is committed to protecting your privacy. Our Privacy Policy is available online at www.eHarlequin.com or upon request from the Reader Service. From time to time we make our lists of customers available to reputable third parties who may have a product or service of interest to you. If you would prefer we not share your name and address, please check here. ☐

SRS09R

You're invited to join our Tell Harlequin Reader Panel!

By joining our new reader panel you will:

- Receive Harlequin® books—they are FREE and yours to keep with no obligation to purchase anything!
- Participate in fun online surveys
- Exchange opinions and ideas with women just like you
- Have a say in our new book ideas and help us publish the best in women's fiction

In addition, you will have a chance to win great prizes and receive special gifts!
See Web site for details. Some conditions apply.
Space is limited.

To join, visit us at
www.TellHarlequin.com.

Silhouette®

Romantic

SUSPENSE

COMING NEXT MONTH

Available August 25, 2009

#1575 BECOMING A CAVANAUGH—Marie Ferrarella
Cavanaugh Justice
Embroiled in a strange case, recently discovered Cavanaugh and homicide
detective Kyle O'Brien is assigned an attractive new partner. Transfer Jaren
Rosetti has a pull on him he can't quite explain. But when the murders hit
too close to home, Kyle will do anything to protect the woman he's come
to need by his side.

#1576 5 MINUTES TO MARRIAGE—Carla Cassidy
Love in 60 Seconds
To keep Jack Cortland from losing custody of his sons to their
grandfather, nanny Marisa Perez proposes a unique solution—a marriage
of convenience. But while passion becomes undeniable between them,
someone close is trying to destroy this family. And no one can be trusted
when the threat becomes murder....

#1577 MERCENARY'S PROMISE—Sharron McClellan
Determined to save her kidnapped sister from Colombian militants,
Bethany Darrow enlists the help of mercenary Xavier Moreno…with a little
white lie. Xavier has a mission of his own, but when he discovers Bethany's
deception, can he manage to trust this woman he's come to care for like no
other?

#1578 HEIRESS UNDER FIRE—Jennifer Morey
All McQueen's Men
When Farren Gage inherits a fortune from her estranged mother, she
also inherits trouble. She is threatened for money by terrorists who
Elam Rhule has come to Turkey to kill, and the two are thrown together
in close quarters, finding it impossible to resist the chemistry they share.
She'll need Elam's help and protection, but will his heart be safe from her?